SPIRIT IN THE RED AMBER

John Gschwend

D1527423

This book is a work of fiction. The characters, incidents and dialogues are products of the author's imagination and are not to be construed as real.

http://civilwarnovel.com

ISBN-13: 978-1481975063

Dedicated to my son, Joshua A. Gschwend,
my faithful first reader

Chapter 1

Flames swallowed the building, an orange inferno. Red-hot timbers withered and crumbled behind the wagon as the man pulled at the stubborn horse. It was hell on earth, nothing shorter. People darted around like rats. Explosions and gunshots rattled the air.

While Rhett Butler threw Scarlett's shawl over the horse's eyes, I closed the restroom door, eased back down the aisle to my seat. I stopped at the fourth row—our row. He was gone. Everyone else was still in his seat, the other nine, but not him. He was gone again.

I opened the door to the lobby. As I stepped into the light, it was like exiting a cave, had to let my eyes adjust. He wasn't there, only a plump girl behind the counter reading a book and chewing gum as if she were mad at it.

"Excuse me," I said. "Did you see an elderly man leave the theater recently?"

She didn't answer nor look up, just pointed at the window. I saw him across the street sitting on a park bench. I started to thank the girl, but didn't. Why bother?

The air was hot and sticky. I don't know why my parents moved us to Arkansas. Most people fled Oklahoma for California during the dust storms, but Pop came east—go figure. I reckon it's better than being in Europe with the Germans running roughshod over everyone. Momma said always look for the good—comes some hard sometimes.

I stood below the marquee of *Gone With The Wind* and looked across the street; there was the old man. He had some sort of tablet in his lap, looked to be writing or drawing. I didn't know where he came by the tablet. He didn't have it when he got on the bus with the rest of the old folks. However he came by it, he was busy doodling or something on it. He had found a good spot for that, under a big shade tree in the park.

I should have been angry at the old rounder, but I couldn't be. He was different from all the rest at the home. He was very old, but his mind was sharp—tongue could be, too. The rest of the folks were content to rock in the shade. He always wandered off. Exploring he called it, a ninety-three-year-old explorer—what a hoot.

I took a liking to him, and I think he liked me, called me a foolish pup. He said he couldn't understand how an eighteen-year-old boy could spend all day looking after glue horses. I grinned thinking about it.

I waited for a horse and wagon to move by—leftovers from his time; then I went across the street. I hated to disturb him; he seemed so content. But the old coot couldn't run off from me every time I took them somewhere. If something ever happened to one of them, they would never be able to leave the home again, and I would be parted from my job.

I moved behind him. I didn't want to frighten him, but I wanted to see what he was writing. He turned the tablet over. "Can't shake you, can I, Pup?"

"How did you know I was behind you?" I sat on the bench beside him.

"It is an old trick I learned from the Quapaw. It is a special sense that you acquire from eating the gesmart plant."

"Really?"

"No, you dumb ox." He slapped my knee. "Your shadow fell over me, and that bushy, red mop of yours casts a shadow resembling a mushroom."

I sure was fond of that old man.

"Where did you get the writing tablet?"

He looked down at it and ran his hands across the cover, a print of an Indian chief. "When I came out here, there was a woman with some younguns. One of them left this tablet and a pencil on the ground when they loaded up in a Ford. It was a new Ford, too." He raised his eyebrows. "Who can afford a new Ford these days?"

"I don't know," I said. "Work's picking up a little, with the war in Europe and all."

"Yeah, 'The War'." He scratched his ear. "You'll be in that war if you're not careful."

"I don't believe Roosevelt will let us be drawn into it."

He laughed, shook his head. "Pup, you don't know a stinkin' thing do you?"

I smiled. I knew it was coming.

"If you'd read the *Gazette* like I do, you would know a little something." He turned, positioning himself better to lecture me. "We can't let all of Europe be conquered by Hitler. We'll go. We'll go just like we did during the Great War. I can see the signs."

I laughed. "You can see the signs?"

He turned even more on the bench and faced me. His face was weathered, looked like a road map. He still had a lot of hair for an old man. It was gray—no, snow white. I believe he still had all of his teeth, something unusual for a man his age. He was always clean-shaven. His eyes were deep blue, blue like the bluest sky. His face was an old man's face, but if you only looked into his eyes, you wouldn't know he was old— they didn't fit his aged face.

"Pup, when they call you to war, you go like a good American, but be ready. War is Hell."

"Didn't Sherman say that?"

He smiled. "Yeah, the bastard, but everyone that has gone to war says it, too."

A black boy across the park kicked a rubber ball and it hit the old man on the knee. The boy froze. He didn't know whether to run or sink into the ground.

"He's not even supposed to be in this park." I started to get up, but the old man grabbed my hand.

He yelled at the boy, "Come get your ball, Son. It's all right."

"Mr. Gillette, that colored boy shouldn't be in this park," I said.

The boy retrieved his ball like a scared dog takes a bone from a stranger. The old man winked and the boy was soon running across the park and out of sight.

Mr. Gillette smiled, said, "Be good to everybody, Pup. It makes the world more tolerable." He spit. "I find it contagious."

"Come on, Mr. Gillette; let's finish the movie," I said as I stood.

"I've read the book."

I extended my hand. "Come on. *Gone With The Wind* is the best movie ever made. I went through some trouble to get permission to bring y'all here."

He slowly looked up at me. "Pup, that's not what it was like during that time, not here, not in Arkansas. The good times weren't that good, and the bad times were worse— much worse."

I sat back down. "Do you remember those years?"

He looked down at his shoes, said nothing for a long time. A cardinal lit on the ground and pecked by his shoes. "Red Eagle," he whispered, but he wasn't really looking at the bird pecking at his feet. He was lost somewhere else. He stared at the ground for a long time after the bird had flown.

"Mr. Gillette?"

He said nothing. Maybe this old man wasn't as sharp as I had thought. I reckon at his age your mind can play a lot of tricks on you. I reckon your mind just takes a break every now and then. I took his arm. "Mr. Gillette, let's go back into the movie house."

He suddenly looked at me with those deep blue eyes. They were young—very young and alive. "Pup, I remember those times real good."

I sat back down.

"We lived on the White River just south of DeValls Bluff. The river flowed out of the Ozarks nothing more than a big stream, but by the time it passed through the prairies and bottoms a heading to the Mississippi, it was a sure nuff river. There was always boats a going and coming up and down."

"I didn't know you were originally from Arkansas?" I said. For some reason I thought he was from up north.

"My mother was from New York, my father from here."

"Well, let me ask..."

"Pup, shut up, and let me tell you my story."

I smiled and shut up.

"My mother's family knew Audubon in New York, and we had a collection of his bird prints. I fancied myself an artist, and I wanted to be like him." He smiled. "I remember it well."

Chapter 2

I had a favorite spot on the bank of that old river; that was, when the river was low. Willows draped over a sandbar, creating a cool cave. I could sit there for hours, and did too. I'd draw and just sit around and think. My pa called it slacking; Momma called it reflecting. I had a sweet momma.

My brother, Jacque, understood my drawing, said I was an artist, but he wasn't there. He was killed at some place in Tennessee that I have never heard of, can't even remember the name now. He had joined the Confederate Army at the first. He was a fool—they all were fools, North and South, but we didn't know it then. Both sides were right—both sides were wrong, depended on who you were talking to at the time—or even talk to now. By the end of the war, no one gave a damn. Everyone with any brains was glad it was over, unless you was one of those rich planters that lost all your slaves.

That June in 1862, I was only fifteen. I didn't want to fight in no ridiculous war. My brother was dead, and my sister, Agnes, was married to a Northerner in New York. My folks only declared allegiance to our farm along the White River; no North, no South. We just wanted to be left alone. But you know what:? War don't allow that.

The river ran fast in front of my sand bar, but it appeared to move slow like molasses down hot cakes. The only way you could really tell was to pick out a floating log or something and gauge it as it traveled by, or get out in the river yourself.

I was nestled under my willows, like a rabbit backed up in a briar patch, putting the likeness of a yellow bird called a prothonotary warbler on my pad that evening. It was just before dark, as I recall it now; the owls were starting to scream—you know those ole owls that can scream like a woman. Barred owls they're called.

Like I said, Momma's family was acquainted with the Audubons in New York. That's where my mother was from. My pa stole her away and brought her here along the banks of the White in the wilderness of Arkansas. He was from here. In fact, his father was a Frenchman who settled close to the Arkansas Post and stayed when the rest of his countrymen pulled out.

Jacque and I loved to admire Momma's collection of Audubon's paintings. That's where I took up the notion of being an artist. Jacque had, too, but he wasn't good as me.

That prothonotary warbler was a flitty little bird, and he would not hold still long, so I had to get a picture in my head so I could put it on paper. I didn't want to kill my subjects and then draw them as Audubon had. The warblers nested in a hollow stump. As they came and went, I snatched a draw here and a sketch there. I'd paint my subjects later. That's how Audubon had done it, too.

That's what I was doing that evening when I first saw him. At first I thought it was a log floating down the river; they do that often. It was too narrow for a skiff, so I didn't pay it no never mind.

It was getting fairly dark, and the warblers had stopped coming and going, so I was fixin to pack it in as the crickets and frogs were having high carnival. The moon was full, so the river didn't know if it wanted to be brown or orange or silver. It was that special time, not day, not night, but something all to itself.

That log was moving to my side of the river. That's when I realized it was no log after all. It was a lone man in a pirogue, and he was paddling to my sandbar. I was about twenty yards from the river's edge, and that pirogue slid onto the sand just a rock's throw from me.

A man stepped from the boat, and I hunkered down like a quail. The man came close to my willows, looking around and as alert as a gray squirrel on the ground. This was no regular man—he wasn't white, and he was no Negro. He climbed the bluff bank, just feet from where I's hid like a scared girl. He went to a big, red oak and shimmied up it like a coon. When he was up about fifteen feet, he stopped and poked his hand into a big hollow. He pulled something out and stuffed it into a pouch that was hanging from his side. Then he slid down the tree quieter than any coon I'd ever heard.

I was scared, and I don't mind telling you. Something didn't seem right about this man. What the hell was a grown man doing climbing a tree?

The man slid back down the bank and headed back toward the boat; then he stopped next to my willows. The moonlight covered him like a dim torch. It was an Indian. There were things hanging from his ears, and his hair was long. It was a bona fide, real, wild Indian.

I was told there were no wild Indians left in Arkansas.

They were moved to the West. I thought right then and there: to hell with that—there was one standing right there, and he looked wild as a ten-point buck.

The Indian raised his head and sniffed the air, just like I'd seen a doe deer sniff. He was so close I could see his nostrils flare. Slowly he turned and looked right at me; his eyes looked like black pearls with the moonshine kicking off them. I was as still as a prairie chicken with a hawk above. I don't think he saw me, but he knew I was there. You don't have to see a skunk to know he's there. He looked down at the sand; he was looking at my tracks, I was sure. Next, he looked up at the moon for a spell. I didn't know if he were praying or wanting to howl; made no sense to me, but what did I know about Indians. Then he moved back to the pirogue. As he stepped in, he looked back toward me for a brief second; then he was in the current and soon gone.

I grabbed my tablet and eased from my hiding place. I studied his tracks in the sand and mud—no heel. I looked up at the hollow in that oak. What was he after up there?

Suddenly I was scared. What if he had just gone downstream and landed again, planning on doubling back. I heard that's what those savages would do. I lit out for home faster than a swamp rabbit with a briar in his tail.

I jumped the split-rail fence and landed right in the middle of a cow patty. We only had two cows now, but they messed enough for a small herd. Sometimes I wished the bobcats would eat them like they ate our chickens.

I could see Pa through the window. He was sitting at the table eating. That meant I was late for supper again. He'd be hot. I opened the door and he cut a burning look at me.

Momma cut it off before it started as she moved past him and set my plate on the table. "Where have you been?"

"I saw a real, wild Indian down at the river!" I said as I threw my leg over the chair and plopped down.

"Oh, Johnny, will you ever grow up?" Momma said, ladling beans onto my plate.

"No, I'm square! He came down the river in a canoe and pulled—"

Pa dropped his fork into his plate with a clank and stared at me.

"Pa, I really saw an Indian."

"What were you doing down at the river? You were to hoe the corn."

I just looked at him and said nothing. I had learned a long time ago to lay the shovel down when the hole was already dug.

"Did you hoe the corn, Son?"

Momma moved away to the other side of the table from me. She knew what was coming.

"No, sir; I didn't."

Pa slapped the table so hard the candle fell over. Momma quickly righted it.

"What were you doing, Son, that was more important than tending to our corn?" He scooted his chair from the table. "What in God's green world is more important than making sure we have food to get us through the winter?"

I looked at him with the saddest eyes I could produce. I hoped I looked like a whipped hound. I said nothing.

"Sixteen. You are sixteen and you show no responsibility at all."

I said nothing. I sure wasn't going to correct him—I was still fifteen.

He looked over and saw my drawing tablet on the table. The vein on his forehead swelled up like a little snake as his face grew red.

Momma was ready to catch the candle again.

"Mr. DeView got word today, Johnny," he said as he pulled my tablet to him. "Frankie is dead."

I swallowed. Mr. DeView was our closet neighbor, and Frankie was his only remaining son. He was only seventeen and my best friend He had caught a riverboat four months ago and joined the army.

"He died somewhere in Virginia," Pa said. "I never liked this war, but Frankie did what he thought was right, and he was a man about it."

Momma put her hand over her mouth and sat down beside Pa. She hadn't heard the news before now.

My heart was heavy as lead and my lips trembled. He was my best friend, and now I would never see him again.

Pa looked down at the tablet, tore the drawing of the warbler from the pad. "He's dead for being a man, a man with conviction, and you are out drawing pictures of birds."

"Phillip, you shouldn't talk to him like that," Momma said.

He turned toward her. "Mary."

She said nothing else.

He turned his attention to the drawing. The vein was still there. He glared at the paper. I said nothing. I had never seen him so angry. I wished I would have hoed every cornfield in Arkansas. He touched the paper to the candle, but before the flame could catch he pulled it back, wadded it, and tossed it across the room. He got up from the table and went out the door.

I dropped my head down to my folded arms and wept. I cried for Frankie, and I cried because Pa had always been proud of my art.

Momma came around the table and hugged me. "Son, he doesn't mean it. He's just upset. I'm sure he's thinking about our own Jacque, too." She stroked my hair. "You go up to bed. He will be better tomorrow."

***

The next morning before daylight, I woke up with the only rooster the critters hadn't eaten. I threw on my clothes and went out the window. It was easy to climb down the second story; the chimney and logs made a good ladder. The sky was just purple in the east, but I didn't care if it was black dark; I intended to be in the cornfield before Pa left the house.

I went into the barn to get a hoe. I didn't like Pa being that upset, and I aimed to fix that problem quick. Our barn was big. Grandpa had built it years ago when he moved over from the Arkansas River. Pa had said Indians helped him build it. When weather was bad, it was big enough for our two horses and two cows. We kept a wagon in there, too.

Suddenly an animal jumped off the wagon and ran to the far wall. It scared the fool out of me—probably a coon or possum. I grabbed the hoe and went over to look for it. Pa had said kill them all before they killed the last chicken. It was still fairly dark, but I could see good enough to get a whack at it when it moved. It looked like it ran under one of the old pirogues we had stacked against the wall.

Wait a minute... There was only one pirogue. Where was the other one? They had been Grandpa's. We didn't use them—we had a big skiff for the river.

The Indian!

I dropped the hoe and cut out for the house. "Pa! Pa! That Indian I saw yesterday got one of the pirogues!"

I ran into Pa as I rounded the porch.

"What are you doing, boy? You 'bout near knocked me over."

"One of our pirogues is gone! I bet that Indian took it."

He looked toward the barn. "What Indian?"

"The one I told you about last night at supper." Suddenly I remembered supper and how angry he had been. I hoped it wasn't going to spill over.

He looked at me, then started for the barn. He opened both doors wide to let more light in. The coon shot between our legs. Pa kicked at it, but it was faster than a wet rat.

Pa went to the far wall. "Well, I be blamed," he said. "It is missing."

I gave a weak smile, still remembering last night.

"You saw an Indian?"

"Yes, sir, and he paddled up in a pirogue. Looks like it was ours."

Pa ran his hand across his beard. "Might have been one of them Cherokee Indians down there near St. Charles."

"I don't think so, Pa. This Indian was a real Indian."

Pa grinned. I was glad to see it.

"What is a *real* Indian?" he said.

I blushed. "I mean he was a wild Indian. He had long hair and rings hanging from his ears. He had on moccasins, too. Pa, he acted wild."

Pa opened up the big window in the back to let in the dawning light. "Look around and see if anything else is missing."

We looked that old barn over like we was looking for the old hen's nest, but we found nothing else gone.

I told Pa about the Indian climbing the tree and everything. I don't know if he fully believed me, but he didn't call me no liar, so that there was a positive far as I could tell.

We looked all around the farm, but we could see nothing else queer. It made no sense. Why would a savage come up to the barn and steal an old pirogue when our skiff was tied down on the river? No tools were missing. Nothing seemed swiped out of the garden, except what the critters had bit on. Pa said it was queer indeed.

Now Momma, that was another story all together, I tell you. She believed me, no doubt. I had to describe that Indian down to the last hair. She made sure Pa kept the old musket loaded at all times. She hadn't been that nervous since that big old bear got the calf. I reckon it was just the Yankee blood in her.

We spent the rest of the day in the cornfield hoeing and talking about the Indian. Pa speculated it was probably one of them Indians at St. Charles trying to live like the old days. I told him I didn't think so, and so the day went. All I know is that Indian drew Pa's anger away from me. For that, I was thankful to him.

***

About a week later I was behind the barn repairing the old chicken pen. Pa and Momma had gone up the river that morning to get a couple of hens from Mr. McQuire. Pa was bound and determined to outfox the fox...and coons and possums and minks and on and on. Yeah, good luck.

Well, my mind was on the Indian—seemed like that's all I thought about since that evening. My chores suffered, and my art did, too. I thought about that Indian taking the pirogue, and that got me to thinking about the other pirogue in the barn.

I pulled it out in the sun where I could give it a good once over. It was about twelve feet long, just a dug out cypress log, but I could tell pride went into the making of it. I went to the river, fetched a bucket of water, and spent the next hour cleaning the old canoe. It had two seats cut into the boat. They were like flat humps in the otherwise flat bottom, one close to the rear, the other a quarter from the front. Carved into the rear seat were my grandfather's initials: *C G*, Charles Gillette. Beside them was a little carving, looked like some kind of bird. It was faded and worn—a hawk or eagle, maybe. The boat had one-inch-diameter sticks driven in it from wall to wall, one about a foot from the front and one just behind the rear seat, handles I reckoned.

It would be another couple of hours before the folks got back to the place, so I took the pirogue to the river. I borrowed one of the oars from the skiff and shoved out into the river. I flipped it over first thing. It rocked like a drunk

Indian—I'd heard Mr. McQuire say that. I realized it would not handle like the skiff, no keel, and it was narrow as a garfish. I pulled it to the bank and rolled the water out. This time I paid more attention to balance. Soon I was gliding up and down the edge of the river like an old French trapper. But the test would be to see how it handled the current.

I went for it.

The current caught me like a wind catches your hat. I panicked at first, but soon had the little boat parallel with the current. I moved like an arrow. I got my nerve and made a big arc and went into the current. I was surprised—the pirogue went against the current much better than I had thought it would. Oh, it was still hard, but it was manageable, much more so than the big ole skiff.

I had a high time. I fancied myself a great explorer or wild Indian or mountain trapper. I darted between log snags, zoomed under overhanging willows. I'd gotten right smart with the little pirogue. I reckoned this sort of business was just in my French blood.

I was about a half mile downriver from the farm when I pulled into shore to pee. The river was low so there was a sandbar below a bluff bank. In that bank were holes. Soon I saw a kingfisher shoot in with a small fish. I stood there for an hour watching them come and go like bees to a hive. I had to draw it. I'd come back the next day.

I headed back to the farm. With the way the pirogue cut the water, no doubt I would beat the folks home. I would have the boat in the barn and the coop finished in plenty of time.

***

I woke up late the next morning, and by the time I went outside, Pa had a brush pile burning. He told me to tend it; he and Momma were going to the store at DeValls Bluff, some kind of meeting about the war and the Yankees in Northern

Arkansas.

They weren't gone thirty minutes, and right off the reel I was already tired of tending the fire. Fires were fun when you wanted to mess with one, but when your mind was on something else, they were just another form of work.

I was thinking about those kingfishers down the river. I sure wanted to get down there and sketch them, and I knew if I waited too late they'd be all done feeding. Birds like to do the feeding early.

Pa wanted me to feed the fire a few sticks at a time and keep the flame small. He said not to put too much on at a time, said it could get away from me and burn the farm down. He always treated me like a dumb child. Land sakes, anybody could watch a fire.

The more I thought about the river, the more I wanted to pull foot and head downstream. I got me an idea: I took me a hoe and cleaned all the grass and debris from around the brush; then I made about six small piles. I connected these small piles with a few sticks and leaves. I figured when a pile caught good and got to blazing, it would catch the sticks and leaves and move over to the next pile—kinda like a fuse. My thinking was that by the time it jumped to the next pile the last one would have burned down. It would work like a chain.

When I pulled the canoe into the river, my second pile was just catching. It was going to work like a calf sucking, and Pa wouldn't know a thing. I would be home before him and I would rake all the ashes together, and he wouldn't know no better. I was smart as a steel trap.

***

The pirogue floated on the water like a duck. I could feel the water as it swooshed by. In the little boat I became part of the river, not just bobbed around in it like in a tub. I felt like an otter or a beaver. I soon learned to maneuver the little boat like it was part of my body—oh, what a capital feeling.

I could smell the river. It had a smell all its own: a mix of mud, flowers, trees, dead fish, and other stuff all mingled in. Oh, how I loved it so. I still love it to this day.

I felt free. I felt all grown up.

I pulled into the shore as a kingfisher was squirting out of the hole. I sat on the log I had scoped out and was soon lost in my sketching. It was wonderful. The birds paid me little attention as they came in with their beaks full of little fish. I concentrated hard on the colors of the birds and all the surroundings. I would have to recall it later when I put the paint to canvas.

I was focused on the birds when a big snapping turtle surprised me, and I liked to messed myself before I realized what was about. I grabbed up a gnawed up beaver stick and stuck it at one of his eyeballs. He grabbed it faster than a chicken can peck a frog. If they latch hold of your finger, they won't let go until it thunders; least ways, that's what I always was told. I don't see no reason to doubt it none. We played tug of war for a spell. That's why I didn't see the fisherman when he pulled up on shore.

"Boy, you better let that snapper be before he bites your talliwacker off. Them rascals can be savage as a meat ax."

I turned to see an old man in buckskin. I don't believe I ever saw a nastier looking human before or since. He was big, had long, gray hair and a long beard. They both appeared to be oiled with something.

"When you get done boogerin' around with him, I'd like to fetch him for vittles," he said as he stepped from his boat. He was barefooted as a monkey.

At first I was a little scared, but he smiled, and I could see right off he was the friendly sort.

"I reckon I'm done with him," I said. I backed away with hands spread.

He laughed a big, deep, belly laugh and grabbed the turtle

by the tail. When he hefted the creature, it hissed and a made a low growling sound.

"Whoa," he said. "I be hanged if he don't want to devour me instead."

I backed away a little farther.

"Come here, boy, and hold this creature while I get my knife."

Now I was in a situation. If I didn't grab the turtle, I was a flicker. If I grabbed it, I was a fool. I hesitated not knowing what to do.

"Come now, boy, he's a getting heavy, indeed."

I eased my hand just below his and took hold of the turtle. He let go and the turtle almost went to the ground. He was a heavy critter. But before I could say a word about it, the man had stuck my beaver stick at the turtle. When the beast chomped onto the stick, the man pulled a long knife from his belt, stretched the stubborn turtle's neck, and whacked the head clean off.

"Now, hand me that animal before you get blood all over your boots." The man tossed the turtle into his boat, then bent down and washed his hands and knife in the river. He didn't turn toward me. "What you doing fooling around on my sandbar for?"

I didn't say anything. I didn't know what to say.

He put his knife away and turned toward me. He had a big grin on his face. "Don't worry, boy; I ain't the mean sort."

I felt more at ease. "I'm an artist." I pointed toward my tablet. "I've been drawing the kingfishers living in that hole." I nodded my head toward the burrow.

He looked at the burrow, then walked over to my tablet. "Well now, that's some pumpkins." He was very careful not to drip water on the paper. "You drawed that all by your lonesome?"

"Yes, sir. I did."

He looked up at me, then back down at the drawing. "That's mighty fine doodling, I tell you."

"Thank you."

He kept looking at it and nodding his approval.

"My name is John Gillette."

He suddenly looked at me and gave me a strange stare. He looked me up and down, then back to the tablet. "Well, you are a good drawer, John Gillette. You can do a right smart job." He smiled again, then walked to the pirogue. "Where did you come by this?"

"It was my grandfather's."

"Well, I be damned." He looked the pirogue up and down. "Yessir, I be damned, Quapaw trimmings and all."

I said nothing, but I immediately thought about the Indian I had seen. Suddenly I felt a strange chill run over me.

He went to his boat, turned back. "You want a couple catfish?"

"No, thank you."

He shoved back off into the river and started paddling. He turned back. "Be careful on the river, John Gillette; never know when them Yankees will be coming up." With that he was gone, and I didn't get his name.

I grabbed my tablet and boarded the little boat. Now, all I could think about was the Indian. I stroked the paddle in the current and thought I saw the Indian behind every tree.

All of a sudden the Indian didn't matter anymore. Now my mind was only on the black smoke toward the farm. I had been gone way too long.

***

Pa was throwing water on the chicken house when I ran up to the barn. Momma was beating down the last flame with a broom. There was very little left. The new hens were dead; so was the old rooster. My plan didn't work out.

Pa ripped the tablet from my hand and backhanded me so

hard I hit the ground.

"Phillip!" Momma said.

With a measured tone, Pa said, "All you had to do was watch the fire, nothing more."

I rubbed my jaw, but said nothing. I knew better.

"You piddle around the place like you don't have care in the world, while men are dying in this blasted war." He looked at the ashes, then looked toward the river. "The Yankees are just up the river at Jacksonport. The only railroad in the state is right here at DeValls Bluff." He turned back to me. "Do you understand what sort of situation we are in?"

I was beginning to. The White River flowed into the Mississippi. Yankee gunboats could steam right up the river past us to link up with the Yankees at Jacksonport, and the two armies would both want the railroad. We were too close to the river and the railroad. The war was coming to our doorsteps.

Pa looked down at my tablet. He immediately tore it to pieces. He turned back to me. "I catch you drawing again, I'm gonna beat the hell outta you." He turned and went to the house.

Momma grabbed my hand and helped me to my feet. She dabbed at my busted lip with her apron. "You know he didn't mean to hit you."

I thought how ridiculous that was. Of course he meant to hit me because he did hit me.

"He's scared, Johnny. He just wants to stay out of the war, but he's afraid it won't let us."

I looked down at my tablet. It was the second time he destroyed my work. I was determined it would be the last.

"Johnny, you've seen the Confederate gunboats up and down the river. When we went to the meeting on the war, there was a man there that had just come from Kentucky. He said the Yankees had many, many gunboats. He said the little

Confederate fleet didn't stand a chance."

I wasn't worried about no gunboats. All I could think about was Pa destroying my tablet.

"They will come right up that river soon, Son."

I absently looked toward the river.

"We will see the smoke billowing from those devilish stacks, and there is nothing we can do about it," she said. Then softly, she said, "My people, Johnny, my people."

The pain in my face ran away. It was immediately replaced by a pain in my heart—my poor mother. I hugged her.

"Some at the meeting said the Northerners are too soft." She wept. "Oh, Johnny. Oh, Johnny. They don't know. They just don't know."

I wept with her.

***

That night as I lay stretched out on my bed and listened as owls called to each other. I always tried to identify the night birds, whippoorwills and such.

I used to guess what riverboat was coming and going on the river, the *Mary Patterson*, the *S. H. Tucker*, or maybe even the Confederate gunboat, *Maurepas*. There were many more, but lately there wasn't much happening. I reckon it was because the Yankees were at Jacksonport upstream.

That old river was a highway. The Indians used it, then the French, then Americans, now we Confederates. In my short life I'd seen all kinds of boats on it—canoes, rafts, keelboats, flatboats, and the king, steamboats. I'd always wanted to travel on it. The farthermost I'd ever been was downstream to Crockett's Bluff, and that wasn't nothing but a jump.

I got up and looked out the window. I could see the river with the moon on it. It was smooth as a flat stone. I could let my mind run and see an old French trapper stroking against the current, making his way all the way up to Missouri. I could imagine a small fleet of Quapaws or Chickasaws returning from the mountains with bear pelts stacked in their canoes. A mind is magic; it can take you anywhere.

Suddenly, I heard Momma and Pa arguing downstairs. It was strange—they never fought. I put my ear to the floor.

"His art doesn't hurt anything," Momma said. "He is so very good at it."

"I ain't spending no more money on that waste," Pa said. "There is no way to get that paper and stuff, anyhow, no matter how much money we have. The damn Yankees have got us bottled up."

"Phillip, please let the boy be."

"I am firm. If I catch that boy doodling again, I will whip the tar out of him. Tomorrow I aim to get rid of all that trash, so his mind will be away from it."

I heard the last sentence clear from the window. Pa had opened the front door. I went to the window.

"Where are you going?" Momma said.

"The boys are down to Frank's barn. We are going to discuss our strategy for when the Yankees come. My strategy tonight is at the bottom of a bottle." He slammed the door.

I went downstairs.

Momma wiped her eyes. "Johnny, you should be asleep."

I went to her and took her hand. "What's the matter with him, Momma?"

We sat on a bench by the door.

"He's afraid, Johnny. He's afraid for us and the place."

"We have an ace, Momma; you're from New York."

She smiled. "If that card worked, Son, I would end the war tomorrow."

"But surely the Yankees won't attack innocent civilians." I said.

"Johnny, when we were at DeValls Bluff, we heard the Yankees had Hessians in their army at Searcy. It was reported they were preying on civilians."

"Germans?"

"At this point we don't know what is truth and what is not. Your father is afraid for us and the farm."

***

Pa came home about two hours later. When I knew he was asleep, I slipped out the window. I had with me my three remaining tablets and my pencils. I had already sneaked down and got a little food. I eased the barn door open, dragged the pirogue from the barn and placed my stuff in it. I reached behind the door and grabbed my fishing pole. The pirogue was long so I had plenty of room for my bag of clothes, art supplies, fishing pole, and blanket.

I dragged the boat down to the river, took the paddle from the skiff, and shoved into the water. I looked back at the house and farm. I hoped Momma would understand. I loved my art, and I couldn't stand for Pa to destroy anymore of my work. Maybe he would understand, too.

I nosed the boat into the river. I had no plan and very little money. The adventure would be like art—it would develop as I went along. There had to be more to life than a farm below DeValls Bluff, Arkansas. I was young. I didn't know no better because I knew everything.

Chapter 3

The river was lonely. The river would be my friend for a while. How long, I did not know. My plan—if I really had a plan—was to make it all the way to the Mississippi, then go back up the Arkansas. I would catch my food from the river, and with the little money I had, I would buy the few supplies I would need. I would take it one day at a time.

I pulled into the bank where the kingfishers had their burrow. I started fetching driftwood and sticks, and soon had a little fire going. Come daylight I would begin drawing the birds again. Pa would not destroy my work this time. I smiled at that—I was my own master.

It was pushing a full moon, so I could easily see to gather the wood I would need to keep the fire stoked all night. I placed my blanket close to the fire and mounded up sand for a pillow below the blanket. It was comfortable.

I settled in my bed and looked at the stars. Even with the

bright moon, I could see billions of them. I didn't know how to navigate by the stars, but I appreciated that people can and have. Sailors have sailed around the world just by looking at the stars.

Suddenly a shooting star streamed across the sky, orange at first, then turning to greenish-white, then broke into pieces and fizzled out like fireworks. Another, then another farther away streaked through the heavens. It was grand, I tell you.

Crickets and frogs sang in the woods, like so many musical instruments. A nighthawk dove close to the fire after moths. Soon small bats did the same.

The river had a low, smooth song as it flowed by. Fish flounced and skipped every now and then. I thought about how far that water had come. I had never been up in the Ozark Mountains, but that's where the river comes from. I had heard it was clear as well water up in those mountains. I dreamed of going up there some day—after the war and the Yankees were whipped.

I looked for the big dipper, then the little dipper. Oh how pretty those stars were—like jewels. I reached my hand up and pretended I could pluck them from the heavens like so many grapes.

I heard a lone wolf call way off in the distance, probably over on the prairie. It didn't scare me at all. It was soothing. A little later another answered. I reckoned they were talking to each other. The prairie had probably heard that song for thousands of years.

I knew I needed to sleep, but I just couldn't take my eyes away from the stars. I looked for the North Star and found it in the little dipper. They say the North Star is the one to guide you—it never moves in the sky as the others.

The French trappers came right up this river. I bet they used the stars to help them as they traveled through the prairies and mountains. I bet they especially used them when they got in the big woods along the river. Some of those trees are so big and full they block out the sky. It is plumb dark under them during mid-day. I'm sure the trappers would just find a clearing somewhere, find the North Star, and move right along.

I know the Indians used the stars, too. They didn't have a compass, so they had to use the stars. This river was a highway for the Indians when they were here, but now they are...

I suddenly remembered the Indian in the pirogue. I noticed I no longer heard the crickets or the frogs, only the smooth swoosh of the river as it crawled by. It's queer how things can get quiet and you haven't even realized the change.

I brought no weapon—what an idiot.

Everything was a silver glow under the full moon. I could see a far distance down the sandbar, and there was no way anything could sneak up on me without me spotting it first. If something charged at me from the woods, it would be a different story.

I was thinking the best thing for me to do was get back in my boat and shove off. But I would be thinking about the Indian every time I stopped. I might as well go back home if I was going to do that.

I found a pointed stick that I had piled up for firewood. It would be my weapon.

I sat by the fire and tried not to think about the Indian. Pa was right; the Indian was probably a local from St. Charles. He may even be from over on the Arkansas River. For some reason the fire was comforting. Fires are funny that way.

A lone bullfrog off in the darkness started up with its deep bellow, "Jug-O-Rum, Jug-O-Rum." Another answered, "Knee-Deep, Knee-Deep." Then all at once, all the other smaller frogs started at the same time. The crickets wouldn't be outdone, so they chimed right in. My orchestra was back to full flow. It put me at ease, and I looked for the North Star again.

***

The next morning I awoke at the crack of dawn with a start, as men in a flatboat yelled at me. They looked like Confederate soldiers. I stood and waved back at them as they floated on by. They appeared to be in a hurry.

I soon heard the chatter of the kingfishers as they became busy feeding the young in the burrows. I grabbed my stuff and got to the job of sketching them. At first they were skittish and didn't want to go to the burrow with me sitting in the open. I moved back a piece, and they grew comfortable. I sat there for a couple of hours and soon had the likeness I wanted on the paper and in my mind. When I got back to the paints, I would have no problem.

I've always had a great memory. I think I'm gifted. Momma said I've always been that way, even as a nubbin. I never misplace anything. I always remember dates and times. I would have no problem remembering the colors of my bird subjects when time came to put the color to them.

I gathered my stuff into the pirogue and shoved off. I didn't know where my next stop would be and didn't give it a care. I had looked at Pa's map before, and I knew every town on the White and Arkansas. I had a good idea the distances between the towns and steamboat landings. Oh, what an adventure this was going to be.

I knew the call of most birds. I would listen; if I heard a particular bird, I would go there and investigate. It was nesting season, so I should find many subjects for my art.

The river had all sorts of streams and bayous that emptied into it. I could travel right up them. I would explore like Lewis and Clark or Pike, maybe even De Soto. I would do whatever I wanted, and no one would stop me.

I found one such slough about fifteen minutes after I left

the kingfishers. It was a slow lazy creek bordered by giant cypress trees. I nosed the little boat into it and paddled on. It was dark there, not bright like out in the river. The water looked black. It had a smell to it—not a stink—but not flowers, either, more of a fishy smell. The water was alive with movement. Bass and perch swirled and splashed among the cypress knees. Those spider-looking bugs slid across the surface of the water. I never understood how they did that without sinking.

Birds sang everywhere. The trees were alive with them. I knew them all: different warblers, vireos, gnat-catchers, fly-catchers, wood ducks. Suddenly I heard the tooting call of the ivory-bill woodpecker, sounded like a small horn. I put my hand to my ear. Yes. It was no doubt. I wanted to draw the giant woodpecker, "The Lord God Bird."

I stroked the pirogue farther down the bayou. The big bird appeared to be feeding, then flying farther down the creek. It seemed to be leading me like you lead a horse with an apple. Then it suddenly turned away from the bayou. I pulled my boat to the bank and grabbed my tablet and pencil from the leather bag and headed toward the calls. I took notice where the sun was so I didn't get turned around when I went to find my boat again.

I found the woodpecker—in fact, I found two. It was a nest cavity, and it was as busy as the kingfisher burrow. The birds were in and out of the hole like squirrels in a hollow gum. I backed off and found a log to sit on. I was drawing before my butt settled good on the green moss growing on the log.

Now, ivory-bill woodpeckers are big—big like a small duck, and when they peck on a tree it sounds like an ax whacking it. They came in tooting and chattering with a ruckus. A body could hear them a mile through the woods. I had to slow myself down. I was drawing too fast. I've always been in too big of a hurry. I had to pace myself to get the perfect likeness on paper. Unlike the kingfishers, which brought beaks full of little fish, these woodpeckers had spiders and big grubs. I couldn't tell what else, but I could see things squirming. The chicks in the cavity liked it all; I could hear them chirping when the parent woodpecker would land outside the hole. It was a capital experience, all in all.

I had the birds sketched out pretty good, but I didn't have the tree detailed, yet. It was a good tree, with a lot of character, a great big cypress tree that lightning had struck. You couldn't ask for a better subject.

Suddenly I smelled a strong musky smell. I knew what it was—I had smelled it before. My legs were crossed with the tablet in my lap. I slowly moved the tablet and there it was. A nasty looking cottonmouth snake had coiled up next to my boot. Now this snake is a mean critter. No snake is meaner or will bite you quicker.

I felt the panic growing in me like the head on a pot of beans. If I moved too fast, he would get me, no doubt. I was in a pickle, I tell you. What to do? What to do?

His old tongue flicked in and out like the devil himself. His eyes were mean and nasty. And he stunk. Just when I thought it was as bad as it could get, another one came from under the stump and slithered right between my boots. I almost filled my pants.

Faster than I could possibly tell you, they attacked each other. They got to twisting and squirming and rolling all around my feet. It scared me so bad I fell off the log backwards and was off the ground before the dirt could stick to me.

I grabbed my stuff and struck out for the boat. I thought about other snakes in my path, but I figured I was running so fast that if they struck at me, I would be gone before the fangs opened. I ran so fast I almost slid into the bayou.

My boat was gone!

I was in such a hurry to get to the woodpeckers that I forgot to pull it firmly ashore or tie it. There was a slow current in the slough, and it took the boat.

I struck out downstream. If I didn't catch up to it before it hit the river, I would be in trouble. That old river would take it like the wind takes chaff. I ran faster and faster but saw no pirogue. I could see the river up ahead. That wasn't good.

And to pile on agony, all my stuff was in the boat, even my money. I was as foolish as they come.

I slid to a stop, almost falling on my face. My boat was at the mouth of the slough where it emptied into the river. It was up on the bank. I eased up to it. Someone had dragged it ashore and tied it. I looked around but saw no one. I saw no tracks in the dirt or marks on the bank where another boat may have pulled up. I had more goosebumps than a plucked goose. I felt I could not leave there quick enough.

I put my things in the boat and pushed it out into the bayou. As I paddled it into the river, I turned and looked at the bank and the woods beyond. I could see no one, but my boat didn't tie itself off.

***

The west sky was turning orange; I didn't want to be on the river when it grew dark. I was getting pretty hungry, but I didn't want to stop and fish. I wanted to make it to the town of Clarendon before night. There was a nice place to camp below the town; Pa and I had camped there before. I could buy something to eat in town at Mrs. Flanigan's boarding house. She was a fine cook, but I was so hungry I could have eaten leather.

When I got to where the Cache River emptied into the White, I pulled ashore to relieve myself. I could hardly go for thinking of the incident upriver. I had to stop thinking on it or it was going to drive me crazy.

Just as I buttoned up, two boats came out of the Cache. They had soldiers in them. I waved as they passed. They turned and went downstream on the White. It got me to wondering why all the soldiers were going downriver. Why didn't they go upriver and attack the Yankees around Jacksonport?

The river had changed so. Very few steamboats now. Used to be steamers coming and going all the time. Maybe the war would be over soon and things would get back to normal.

As I started for the boat, I heard the call of a painted bunting in the briar patch up the bank. I ran back to the canoe and grabbed my stuff. Painted buntings get their name because the small male bird looks like someone splashed him with different colored paints: blues, reds, yellows.

I kept looking in the briars and I finally spotted the dull-yellow female sitting on the nest. I didn't want to spook her, so I moved slowly to get set up. It was easy to draw her—she just sat there on the nest. The male was another story. He fluttered around, in and out of the briar patch like a horsefly. He finally spotted me and the scolding was on. The female left the nest and joined in on the bashing. I didn't want to jeopardize the nest so I pulled back. I had enough anyway.

I sat next to the pirogue and fleshed in the drawing. It would be beautiful when I added the paint to it. Birds made fine subjects, so many lovely colors. Each bird had its own personality. What would the world be like without the beautiful birds? It would be a pitiful place.

I wrapped my tablet in the rubber blanket and placed them in the bag. As I slid the boat into the river, I could still hear the buntings fussing from the bank.

***

It was candle-lighting time when I pulled into the shore at Clarendon. I took my bag with me. The pirogue would be fine. No one would take the old, little boat.

Mrs. Flanagan was finished feeding when I arrived, but she let me eat in the kitchen. She was a nice old lady. She was some kind of Indian—Chickasaw, I think. Pa had said her husband had brought her from Mississippi, but he died soon after they arrived at Clarendon.

She had a sixteen-year-old colored boy, Bob, that worked around the place sometimes. He was a friend and he ate supper with me in the kitchen.

"Where bouts you goin,' Johnny?" Bob said, shoveling peas into his mouth.

"Downriver." I grabbed another piece of cornbread and sopped it into the peas.

He took a few gulps of milk, then wiped his mouth with his sleeve. "Downriver don't tell me doodley."

I smiled, but said nothing and kept eating.

"They says them Yankees is comin' down the Mississippi," he said. He stared at me to gauge my reaction.

I said nothing.

"You knows the White River runs into the Mississippi."

I took a big swig of my milk, but said nothing.

He smiled. "That fine, Johnny. You ain't gotta spill nothin' on me."

"Maybe, I'm going to join the Yankee Army."

Bob laughed. "Maybe I'm a joinin' the Sesech Army."

We both laughed.

Mrs. Flanagan entered the kitchen. "What you two boys laughing over?"

"Johnny was telling me a fish story," Bob said and winked at me.

"Johnny, how are your folks?" she asked as she took our plates.

I got up from the table. "They're fine."

"They know where you are?"

"Of course."

She stared at me wanting more. I gave her nothing else.

Bob stood. "I's gonna help Johnny make camp."

As we went out the back door, I heard her tell Bob not to get any bad notions from me, or she would tell his father.

***

Bob had an old beat-up rowboat, and he followed me to the camp just downriver from town. There was a beach there where the odd traveler would spend the night if the weather was fair as it was now. Bob had stolen a few sticks of wood from Mrs. Flanagan's pile and soon had a little fire going.

I've known Bob for a spell. He'd worked up and down the river since he was a squirt. He worked with his father on flatboats and steamboats, doing whatever they couldn't get the white folks to do. Bob's family was the odd lot of Negroes. They were free blacks. Old man Mr. Willard died a few years back, and in his will he set the whole bunch free.

We picked up a few more pieces of driftwood to keep the fire going after the stolen wood was gone. Then we settled in by the fire and caught up on things since we had last seen each other. If there was one thing about Bob, he loved to gab. I had told him I was on a drawing expedition, and he wanted to see my work.

"That there is one big peckerwood," Bob said, as he angled the tablet toward the fire.

"Don't set it afire, Dummy."

Bob moved the tablet toward the fire. "How about that, Cracker?"

"They're gonna find your butt floating down the river face-down."

We both laughed as he moved the tablet back to his lap and turned to the next page.

"Boy, you sho can scribble out a good picture," Bob said as he looked at the kingfishers. "If we wasn't at war with them Yankees, you could go to New York or Boston somewhere and make a shiny dollar with this stuff."

I smiled. Bob may never have left Arkansas, but he had smarts from working on the steamboats. He had seen all sorts.

"You just wait until I put the paint to it, I tell you," I said.

"It'll be sweeter than blackberry pie," Bob said as he handed the tablet back to me.

I placed it back into the bag, and we settled in together close to the fire. It was fine sitting there watching the river flow by and hearing the night birds.

I always liked Bob. He would sometimes spend the night on our farm. He and his father would help us get our crop in. They traveled all over the area working like that. Bob was a friend. He never judged me or thought me odd like others did. He and Jacque were the only two that ever understood my eccentricities. Now with Jacque gone, that only left Bob.

"Bob, how are your folks?"

"They mostly fine. Pa struck out upriver for Des Arc. He heard there was work at a sawmill, but now we is worried with them Yankee's upriver." Bob tossed a stick into the fire and sparkles rose up like red stars. "They says they is a lot of new Confederate soldiers in the state now. I's worried they may take Pa fo a slave or something. They don't know him like everybody else along the river does."

"I'm sure he will be fine. I know he always carries his papers."

Bob smiled and we fell silent. We both ran out of things to say, and Bob was now worrying about his Pa. A bass flounced in the river, running shad. Bob stood. "I reckon I better get back toward Mrs. Flanagan's. It's getting late." He stuck his hand out. I stood and took it. "Wherever you is going, John Gillette, you be careful."

I smiled and nodded.

"I will be workin' for Mrs. Flanagan for a spell. She good

to me. You look me up when you come back, so I knows you is safe."

"I will Bob. I promise."

Soon he and the boat disappeared in the blackness, and I was alone with the busy bass. I pulled my pole from the boat. I would catch that bass for breakfast in the morning. I saved enough firewood to make my breakfast fire. After a belly full of fish, I would shove off to new adventures.

I sat near the fire. There is something about a campfire that makes you want to sit by it and look at it. You watch the flames lick around the logs, and the embers glow and flash. I knew I needed to turn in, but just a bit longer by the fire was soothing medicine.

I began to think about the next day, then the next. What new adventure was around the bend? What new bird would I draw? I was too young and ignorant to think about my next dinner or how and when would I get back home.

Whenever I did eventually make it back to the farm, the painting would begin. I looked forward to that with all my soul. I loved bringing my art to life. It moved me inside. It made my chest heave with pride. If I received much grief from Pa, I would shuck out again. I would—

Suddenly two feet appeared in front of me next to my fire.

I looked up with a start. It was a filthy looking man with a scar across his left eye. The firelight reflected across his face, revealing a nasty grin. The scar looked like a horseshoe.

"How do? Mind if I sit by your fire a spell?" He sat without my reply. I said nothing. He had a giant bowie knife on his belt and a revolver in his hand. "You know it can be a mite dangerous to camp along the river alone." He tapped the revolver on his knee.

I mustered strength and composed myself. "I'm not alone. I have friends, and they will be coming back from town any minute."

"The only friend you have is that darky boy, and he's long gone."

The fear jumped on me like a bad dog. How long had he been watching me, and what was he after?

"You need to be smarter if you're gonna travel the river." He dug in his ear and mined out a nugget, inspected it and flicked it into the fire. "You see, I never travel alone."

Another man stepped from behind me. He wore a Confederate cap, but he was no soldier. He had long, stringy, yellow hair. The man sat on the other side of me.

The man with the scar leaned over to the boat and pulled out my bag. "What do we have here?"

I reached for the bag, but Yellow Hair grabbed my arm.

The man opened the bag and worked my tablet out. "Well, we have some pretty pictures here." He angled the tablet toward the fire and flipped the pages. "You fancy yourself an artist, do you?"

I said nothing. What was there to say? They had me laid bare. They knew it as well as I did.

He flipped the page again, and without looking at me he said, "We will take your money and let you be."

"I have no money."

Yellow Hair slapped me. It was a surprise. It hurt, but it took me awhile to understand what had happened. The blood dripping from my lips, dropping on my leg, brought me to the reality of the situation.

The man ripped a page from my tablet and threw it in the fire. "There weren't no picture on that page, but there will be on the next un."

Suddenly there was a thud, and Yellow Hair fell over on his side. Blood flowed from a pop-knot on his head. There was a big river rock next to the fire—it hadn't been there before.

The other man shot to his feet, waving the revolver in all

directions. "I don't take no shit! I'll kill this boy and anybody else that—"

Another thud and a big rock rolled to my feet. The man dropped the revolver. A red spot appeared between his eyes, and he staggered in place for a spell. Then he collapsed backward like a felled tree.

I jumped to my feet. "Bob? Is that you?"

There was no reply. The bass skipped and flounced in the river.

I reached down and grabbed the revolver. I thought about it and dropped it. I didn't want one of those big rocks up side my head.

The moon was high now. I looked toward the river. I believed it was where the rocks had come from. I saw a raccoon working the river edge for crawfish, but no person. I was more scared now then I was before the rocks.

I felt my skin tingle. Instantly, I knew what they meant when they talked about the hair standing up on the back of your neck. I swallowed hard and slowly turned. There he was.

Chapter 4

It was the Indian.

I was so scared I couldn't run, scream, or mess my pants. He was tall and solid, wore buckskin and some kind of necklace made of shell—mussel, I think. He had earrings, but they looked store-bought. His face was granite and weathered. But he was old with gray streaks in his hair. He was still extremely intimidating.

We stared at each other for a time. Then he bent and grabbed Yellow Hair under the arms and dragged him into the darkness. I could see his silhouette under the moon as he pulled the man behind a big fallen willow and out of sight. He came back and grabbed the other man in the same fashion. I said nothing. He said nothing. He just dragged him behind the willow, too. I heard a few muffled sounds, then silence.

I thought about hurrying the pirogue to the river, but I would never make it before he shot one of those meteors at me. I had seen how that would turn out.

He came back to the fire, had an armful of driftwood, placed a couple of pieces on the fire, then sat next to it and stared into it.

I was left standing there confused. I knew nothing else to do, so I sat across from him. I knew he could hear my teeth chattering. We sat that way for a long time, thirty minutes or so, and said not a word. I looked at him—he looked into the fire, only taking his eyes away when he added more wood. I slowly gained confidence. If he hadn't killed me by then, I must have been in good standing.

I cleared my throat. "I want to thank you for saving me from those thieves," I said, not knowing if he could understand me.

He looked straight into my eyes. He stared for a long time, then nodded one time and went back to studying the fire.

This was a strange situation. I didn't know what to do. "My name is Johnny."

He never looked up, said "John Gillette."

I felt a queer feeling run down my body. I knew nothing of Indians. Maybe he was a medicine man or something. "How do you know my name?"

He slowly looked at me and said nothing for a long time. Then finally he said, "Where are you going?"

I didn't know what to say. I didn't know what to do, but I reckoned it did no harm telling him where I was going, so I did. He could have killed me already if that was his intention. "I'm an artist." I pulled my bag from the boat and handed him the tablet.

He angled it toward the fire. The fire had grown weak so he put a couple of logs on it. Slowly the fire grew and he turned the pages, inspecting my work. He said nothing, nor did he show any change in the expression on his weathered face. He looked at every picture slowly and totally. He inspected it as a lawyer might inspect some important document.

"I will paint them later when I return home," I said.

He nodded and handed it back to me.

We sat there for a time, saying nothing. It was odd. He stared at me. No, he inspected me for a long spell as you would inspect a horse. I didn't know what to say. I was afraid to say anything, to tell the truth. Then abruptly, yet slowly, he rolled over in the sand, made himself comfortable, and closed his eyes.

I knew I couldn't sneak away from him. I was in a fix.

"Who are you?" I blurted. I had not planned saying it. It just fell out.

He never opened his eyes. "You must sleep now. We will go down the river together at first light."

We will go together? What was this all about? I thought about the two thieves. "What about the men you stoned? They may attack us in the night."

"They will attack no one." He didn't open his eyes.

He must have finished them off when he pulled them into the darkness. He had a knife on his side; I wager that is what he killed them with. I didn't see any scalps or blood on his hands, but that was no matter; he could have still cut their throats. That meant he was a murderer. He could have a history of—

"They left awhile ago." His eyes were still closed. "They got in their boat and went downriver."

"How could you possible know this?" Then I remembered him sniffing the air back at the farm when I thought I was hidden from him. Indians are wild like animals. They can hear like animals I supposed. He must have heard them sneaking away in the darkness.

"I put them in their boat and shoved them into the current. They will be miles downstream before they wake up." Again he didn't open his eyes or stir.

"They were still alive?"

"*Oui*. Now you sleep."

Oui? I knew I detected a French accent. I laid down and figured I may as well sleep, but this Indian reminded me of someone. That was odd but I would sleep on it—if that was even possible. *Oui*?

***

When I awoke, he was gone. My pirogue was gone, too, with all my drawings, everything. That stinking Indian had stolen it all.

I yelled out like an idiot, just wasting my breath. I kicked at the sand. There was nothing to do but head toward Clarendon. With no tablet there was no need going on. Oh, what a rotten break it turned into—stinking Indian thief.

I looked up the river and saw what looked like a raft coming. It was an odd looking... It was the Indian. He was in my pirogue. No. He had my pirogue tied to another pirogue, which he was in. I just stood there waiting. What else could I do? Directly he pulled ashore in front of me.

"You stole my pirogue," I said.

He said nothing as he pulled onto the shore.

He had lashed the two pirogues together. They were identical. Then it hit me. "Hey, you stole that pirogue from our barn!"

He checked the cord he had tied them together with. The two boats mated like two peas in a pod. "I did not steal."

"I reckon you did. It's the same one that was in our barn. It was my grandfather's."

He pointed to my pirogue. "That was your grandfather's."

"They were both my grandfather's."

He slid them back toward the water. "Get in."

I looked at him for a short time; then I climbed in my pirogue—no other options that I could see. When he shoved it farther into the water, he climbed in the other and began paddling.

The two little boats mated together like they were built to be together. He had cord tied in the hole in the front and the hole in the back. The holes line up perfectly.

"You paddle, too," he said.

I grabbed a paddle. "Where we going?"

He said nothing. His leather face was firm and determined.

I reckoned I didn't have much of a choice in the matter, so I just kept paddling, and we kept going. I looked over in his boat to see what possessions he had. There was a little bag—the same one he had on his side when he climbed the tree. He had an ax and a fishing pole. I guessed he didn't need much. I didn't know anything about Indians.

We paddled right by the little hamlet of Aberdeen. I don't know why I didn't yell or draw their attention, but I didn't. I really wasn't afraid any longer, figured if he was going to kill me, he would have done so already. I was starting to get curious about where we were going and what we were doing. My adventure had taken a strange turn, becoming high excitement.

About a mile past the town we pulled ashore next to a big tree that had fallen into the river. He stepped out and grabbed his pole from the boat. Then he reached in his bag and brought out some kind of meat, wrapped it into a ball and threaded it onto his hook. He walked onto the fallen tree and dropped his line in the water among the submerged branches. Almost immediately, he came out with a nice size catfish. He knew what he was doing—we wouldn't go hungry.

We soon had a fire going. We ate the fish and some mulberries he had in his bag. He had salt, too, and it went well with the fish.

"What else you got in there?" I said.

"Many important things," he said with that iron face.

"What kind—"

"Private things." He kicked sand into the fire and headed for the pirogues.

He was a very fit man, but he was an old man. His hair was mostly gray, tied in a long queue. He was an Indian alright, but he was not as dark as what I would have expected. His eyes were grayish blue. His face was wrinkled, but he had a young spark in his face and eyes.

I followed him to the pirogues. There was nothing else to do, but follow him. "Where are we going?" I said as we shoved off.

He didn't answer.

We paddled on for a few hours, not talking at all. I didn't feel like a prisoner, but I didn't exactly feel I was free to go either. I wasn't afraid of the man, but I was growing concerned as to where our destination might be.

I studied the two little boats. They were identical—almost. There were grooves carved into the gunwales so the two boats mated together perfectly, and I don't believe it was a coincidence that holes were placed in such a location as to allow the two boats to be lashed together. I had never noticed this about the boats when they were in the barn. To tell you the truth, I wasn't too concerned about the old relics as they lay under dust and spiderwebs.

We drifted by the steep hills at the little town of Crockett's Bluff. That's as far as I had ever been. It would all be new territory for me here on out. I would have to rely on the map or the Indian.

A little time later, the Indian headed the boats into a creek to the left.

"Where are we going?" I said.

He said nothing.

I threw my paddle into the boat. "Am I your prisoner?"

He said nothing; but I did see a small smile cross his lips, but it was fleeting.

I picked my paddle back up and began stroking.

"This will carry us to Maddox Bay," he said.

I turned. I had heard of Maddox Bay. The town of Lawrenceville is on Maddox Bay. "I assume you have a reason for going to Maddox Bay."

The smile was there again, but gone quickly. He said nothing else as we went under over-hanging willows.

The stream was a narrow run with swift water flowing back toward the river. As we kept paddling, it opened up into a vast lake. Wicked-looking cypress trees lined the banks. We paddled for a time and came upon a small shanty. The Indian pulled the boats to a little wharf made of cypress logs with cypress planks across it. He climbed upon it and a cottonmouth slid into the water. It had been hiding behind a small cottonwood tree that was growing between the planks. The Indian tied the pirogues, then went up the bank and into the shanty.

There I was alone. I stepped out onto the wharf, while looking for snakes, of course. Suddenly I had an idea. With the Indian in the shanty, now was the time to make my escape. I grabbed my knife from my bag and went to the back of the pirogues to cut the cord. As I reached in to cut, I stopped. Carved in the back seat of the other pirogue was "JG." I looked back over to the seat on my boat, "CG." What did it mean? "CG" was my grandfather, Charles Gillette. Who was "JG"?

"Well now, if ain't John Gillette the artist."

I turned to see the old man that had killed the turtle on the river a few days back. He was coming down the bank with a musket hanging off his arm.

"What brings an artist like you up to my neck of the woods?"

Before I could answer, the Indian came out the door.

They stared at each other for a long time. It was like they each were looking at a strange creature they had never seen before.

"It's been a long time, Inyun," the man said.

The Indian replied, "*Oui*, very long."

"Why you in my house?"

They seemed to be angry with each other, but I couldn't really tell by the peculiar way they were acting and sizing each other .

"Looking for something to steal, but there is nothing worth taking."

They walked toward each other slowly. They both were old, but I believed they both had fight left in them. The man raised his hand, and then suddenly threw his arms around the Indian. They embraced and patted each other on the back. They embraced for a long time, then slowly pulled away.

"You damn Inyun, I thought you was long dead," the man said.

"*Oui*. I thought the same about you until I found this ragged shack still standing. Anyone else would have torched it long ago."

The man wiped his eyes, smiled and shook his head. "Well, hell, come inside, come inside," he said as he opened the door. He turned to me. "You, too, Little John Gillette."

I walked up the bank. What did he mean, "Little" John Gillette?

Inside of the log shanty smelled like bacon. It was cleaner than I would have guessed, looking at it from outside. It was small—only a bed, a table, couple of chairs and a fireplace. A relic of a bow and old arrows hung from pegs above the fireplace. There was bread on the table, and the Indian and I made short work of it. The man had a pot over a small fire.

"You boys is just in time, just in time for sure," the man

said. "I's got beans a simmerin' with a couple a squirrels tossed in it for good measure."

"Lewis, I hope you cook better than I remember," the Indian said as he shoved the last piece of bread in his mouth.

So the man's name was Lewis. I thought he looked somewhat like a Lewis.

"Well, I reckon that bread didn't choke your red hide none," Lewis said as he stirred in the pot.

The man took three bowls from the shelf—he had but three—and placed them on the table. He filled them with steaming beans and squirrel parts. After he filled mine, he hesitated at the Indian's bowl. "You sure you want any a my beans, Inyun?"

"*Oui, s'il vous plait.*"

Lewis ladled a bowlful. "Damn it, Inyun, stop talkin' that French."

"*Way'-Re-Nah*," the Indian said as he pulled the bowl toward him.

"Damn right you better appreciate it, but don't be talkin' no Quapaw either." Lewis sat down. "It's been years since I talked anything other than English, so don't be throwing it at me."

"*Ca va.*"

"Damn it, John!" Lewis said, then smiled. "You ain't changed a pound."

The Indian didn't smile, just started on the beans.

"John?" I looked at the Indian. "Your name is John?"

Lewis grinned. "You mean you is a travelin' with this here halfbreed, and you don't even know his name?" He slapped his leg. "You don't even know who he is?" Lewis scratched his head. "Are you square, boy?"

The Indian said nothing, and I said nothing.

"Well, now, allow me the pleasure." Lewis cleared his throat, then pointed to me. "John Gillette," now pointing to the Indian, "meet John Gillette."

A thousand things tried to cram through my brain at one time, but the only thing that registered was the "JG" carved in the other pirogue.

Lewis dipped his spoon in his beans and smiled.

"Gillette?" I couldn't think of anything else to say.

Lewis said with a mouth full of beans, "Gillette, that's correct, Gillette."

The Indian—John—just sat there and said nothing.

I faced John. "Are we kin?"

Lewis spit his beans back into his bowl. He wiped his mouth and giggled. "Was your grandfather Charles Gillette?"

"Yes sir, he was."

"Yep, you is kin." Lewis went back to eating his beans, spit and all.

I turned to John. "Why didn't you say anything?" I stood. "You played me for a fool."

"You can't be a fool if you know no better," John said, not looking up from his beans.

"You could have said something."

"It's not my way."

"You hang around him long enough, you will see he has a good many foolish notions," Lewis said.

John turned to Lewis, "De'-Ska."

"Don't call me a cow, you dirty Inyun pig."

John said dryly, "You still understand Quapaw good enough ."

Lewis smiled and finished his beans.

I left the table and went outside. The sun was low and sitting on top the giant cypress trees across the bay. It had turned the water a brilliant orange. A big heron glided down the bay like a kite.

I was confused. I felt betrayed, but I didn't know why. I didn't know the Indian from Adam, but I still felt like he had betrayed me by not telling me who he was.

The door opened and Lewis spilled out onto the little porch sucking on a squirrel leg. I expected the Indian to follow, but Lewis shut the door.

Lewis knew what I was thinking. "He's staring into the fire like an idiot, won't even talk." He pitched the leg bone down into the water.

I turned and looked down at the pirogue, and thought, now would be a good time to leave.

Lewis patted his belly and grunted and spewed. "Love squirrel, don't you?"

The smell was horrible. I went down to the bay.

"You a figurin' on leavin' the Inyun here with me?" he said as he walked down beside me.

I was bracing for the next nasty gassing.

"You won't leave. You have too many questions floatin' in your head." He climbed over into his boat. "Come on, get in."

I hesitated. What was this all about?

He smiled. "Get in, get in. It's too late to strike out anyhow."

"Where we going?"

"We's goin' to run my lines for catfish."

He was right. It was almost dark, so I couldn't leave. I climbed in.

He pulled at the oars, and the wide boat zipped across the water at a good clip. The man was old, but he had no problem handling the boat. The boat smelled like dead fish, and for good reason; there was fish slime in the bottom of it. When we got to the other side of the bay, I saw a line hanging from a willow limb shaking and jerking. A big swirl boiled just under the surface.

"Boy, you know how to run limb lines?" Lewis said.

"Of course. I was raised on the river."

"Yeah, you should know how, being a Gillette."

He maneuvered the boat next to the hanging line, and I grabbed it. The line zipped out of my hand, and Lewis hawed laughing. I laughed, too. The fish was a big one. I grabbed the line again and hauled in a big flathead. When I pulled the hook from the fish's mouth, Lewis handed me a bucket. The stink caught me by surprise.

"What is this?" I said.

"Just cut-up perch."

I pulled a nasty looking piece out and stuck it on the hook. "How long this stuff been in this bucket?"

Lewis pulled at the oars and backed the boat away from the line. "Only a couple of days." It would take that long to get the stink off my hands.

We paddled down the bay to the next line. The bait had been robbed, so I rebaited and we moved on. We caught a few more and had catfish flopping all in the bottom of the boat.

"You will be eating fish for a while," I said.

"I will sell them. I'm partial to turtle meat. Remember?"

I smiled.

"Boy, you really didn't know who the Inyun was?"

I turned in the boat to face him. "No, sir. I had no idea."

He smiled big and looked back down the bay toward his shanty. "I haven't seen him in over thirty-five years." He said nothing else. Soon I could see he was lost in another place, in another time.

"Were y'all friends?"

It brought him back to the present. "Friends?" He belly-laughed. "The Inyun, your grandfather, Paul Sinclare, and me was partners in ever sort of trouble and shine under God's green sky and on His blue grass."

I smiled with him.

"We growed up together, and we roamed the prairie

betwixt here and the Arkansas." He was soon lost again in memory. He kept paddling back toward the shanty, but he really wasn't in the boat with me. He was in some place and time that I could never imagine.

I tried to give him time to come back on his own, but I grew impatient. "What sort of fellow is John Gillette?"

He looked at me and grew serious. "John Gillette is one of the best and truest men I have ever knowed in my sixty-five years." We were getting closer to his shanty. He stared at it. "I would die for him."

That hit me hard. With the way they talked to each other, I didn't expect that. I looked at Lewis's face and noticed his eyes growing wet again. He was still looking toward the shanty. I turned. John Gillette was standing on the porch looking at us. Suddenly I didn't see two old men. I saw two friends.

***

We built a fire and sat there under the brilliant stars. Lewis drank some kind of clear whiskey, but we declined to partake. The night was still and cool. I was thankful for that and thankful for only a few mosquitoes.

Lewis dug around in the coals with a crooked stick. He looked up nervously. I could see something was weighing on him. He looked at John. "What happened to your tribe out west?"

John said nothing as he stared into the fire.

"Me, Paul and Charles started down to the Red River down there in Louisiana, but Paul got sick and we had to turn back. We heard how the Caddo treated your people so bad down there. We heard the Quapaw's corn got flooded out."

"They didn't want my people no more than the white man did."

"We heard your wife died down there," Lewis said. "I'm sorry for that."

John simply nodded.

"Paul had died with the fever, John. Me and Charles went back down there, but your people were so scattered, some with Chief Heckaton, the others with Sarason, others only God knew where." He scratched behind his head. "You knowed we had all moved over here on the White. Hell, you had been here. We figured you would come."

No one said anything for a time.

"Did your mother survive the journey out west?" Lewis asked, then took another drink.

John looked off into the woods, said nothing.

Lewis suddenly threw the bottle into the darkness. "Damn it, John!" He grabbed his stick again and dug hard into the fire, sending up little sparks. "You should have stayed with us. You are half white. You should have stayed. I don't know what to think, you showing back up like this. What the hell do you want? Why are you back?"

"I am *O-Gah-Pah*," John said, but never looked away from the nothingness he was looking at in the dark.

Lewis stopped digging with his stick, said softly, "Yes, you are Quapaw." He nodded slowly and wiped across his face with the back of his hand.

John turned toward Lewis. His eyes smiled. "Mother survived the journey. She lived to be an old woman."

Lewis nodded, smiled.

"Did Paul die hard?" John said.

Lewis began digging in the fire again. "It was rough, but he died like the man he was."

John looked at me, but he was addressing Lewis. "Charles lived to be old, *oui?*"

Lewis looked at me, then back at John. "Charles died about five years ago. He had two sons, Phillip and Jacque."

I turned to Lewis. "Jacque was my brother."

Lewis nodded, then turned back toward John. "Charle's

wife and little Jacque died with the fever. Charles raised Phillip and never got married again." He stretched.

I understood now. My brother Jacque was named after our uncle who died as a baby, and I must have been named after this Indian, but how was he kin to me. I turned to him and he was looking at me.

"Your grandfather was my cousin," John said. I don't know how he knew what I was thinking, but he did.

Lewis looked at John for a long timeand then asked, "How is your family out there in Inyun country?"

John waited a long spell to answer. "It was all confused there, more than it was down on the Red River. My people are strewn all over. When Mother died, I traveled about. I married a Cherokee woman, and we had a son." He said nothing for a time, then began again. "She has been long dead, but my son wanted to fight Yankees. He was killed near Elkhorn Tavern in Northern Arkansas at a big battle just fought up there a few weeks ago. The Indians were fools to take sides in the fighting." He looked off in the darkness. "I had followed to talk sense to him, but he was killed before I could find him. I had nothing left out there, so I followed the White River, and now I am here."

Lewis put a couple more logs on the fire. "Why are you here, John? Why are you really here?"

John didn't answer.

We said nothing for a long time. The owls screamed and bullfrogs bellowed in some slough behind the shanty.

Lewis began laughing. "Inyun, I have to know where you got those buckskins. That ain't Quapaw. I been wanting to ask you that from the start."

John looked down at his pants. A smile grew on his face. It was the first big smile I had seen.

"I traded a revolver I had found on the battlefield to an old German near Batesville."

"Why?" Lewis laughed. "Why would you trade a revolver for old Osage buckskins?"

John's smile melted. "I am sixty-four years old. I don't have time to stop and hunt and make my own clothes."

Lewis stopped laughing. "Why make your own—"

"I am Indian. I am *O-Gah-Pah*," John said suddenly.

"What are you talking about?" Lewis said

John looked squarely at Lewis. "I'm going after it."

Lewis rubbed his whiskers. "After what?" I could tell he knew what.

"*Khi-Dha' Zhu'te.*"

Lewis eased up from the stool and walked toward the bay. "You know we were young then." He turned back toward John.

John said nothing.

I had no idea what they were talking about.

"There is nothing to it. It was all in our young minds."

"Do you have your piece?" John said.

Lewis said nothing for a spell, then suddenly walked into the shanty. He came out with a folded, red cloth. He slowly unwrapped it, revealing a piece of a seashell. In the firelight I could see some kind of art on it.

John smiled. "I knew you would still have it."

Lewis snapped. "It ain't nothin' but a piece of shell. It don't mean nothin' else."

"It held us together. We were strong," John said.

"We were friends," Lewis said. "It had nothing to do with that."

"We were white and black and red, and it held us together like brothers."

"It had nothing to do with it, you foolish Inyun. You came back for this?"

"It had everything to do with it!" John stood. "It is *Wah-Kon-Tah.*"

"I thought you were a Christian," Lewis said.

John said nothing.

Lewis stood looking at John; then he walked over and handed the piece to him. "How many do you already have?"

John admired the piece. He reached in the bag hanging from his side and retrieved a small pouch. He pulled out two more pieces. He sat, and in his lap he put them together like a puzzle. They made a pretty seashell. There was still a piece missing.

"You need Paul's piece," Lewis said as he sat back on his stool.

John studied Lewis. "Where is it, Lewis?"

"I could tell you anything. Paul was a black man. Anyone could have taken it from him. They took his horse. They took his mule. They took his—"

"Where is it, Lewis? Paul would not have let anyone get it. Bad luck follows it, not good."

"John," Lewis pleaded, "why are you doing this?" He stood. "Don't get the boy in this. Go back to where you came from."

"You can go with me, Lewis. We can get it together."

Lewis smiled, reached down and put a couple pieces of wood on the fire. "No. I gave up thinking about it twenty-five years ago. Me and Charles talked about it a few times, but you never came back. Me and Charles drifted apart with time." He looked into the fire for a long spell. "I have a bad back." He looked up but said nothing else.

John wrapped the pieces and put them in his bag. "Where is Paul's piece?"

Lewis took a deep breath and let it out. "There is a large hollow pecan across the river and just below St. Charles. It is buried inside the hollow with gravel scattered over it. The tree has two trunks about halfway up. It is about twenty steps from the river on a small bluff."

John nodded.

"The prairie has changed; many more white people on it. You will have a hard time finding what you are looking for."

"I'll find it," John said as he stood.

Lewis stood and stretched. He went to John and looked into his eyes for a long time. "We waited for you to come back. Even after Paul died we didn't give up hope that we could make a difference, but you never returned." He poked John's chest. "You never came back. Now you show up all these years later. You are a foolish Inyun."

John said nothing, only returned the look.

"Now, we are the only two left, and we have grown old," Lewis said.

John still said nothing.

Lewis relaxed. "I hope you find the *Khi-Dha' Zhu'te*." He offered his hand and slowly John took it. "You foolish Inyun."

***

The next morning John woke me before daylight. When we went down to our boats, Lewis was there placing food into them.

I extended my hand. "It was a pleasure to meet you, Mr. Lewis."

He took my hand in both his. "Little John Gillette, it was a pleasure here as well."

I climbed into my pirogue and waited for John to climb into his.

Lewis placed his hands on John's shoulders. "John, I never forgot you." He sniffed. "I never forgot the four of us. We should have kept our creed. We should have stayed together. Maybe we could have made a difference."

John took hold of Lewis's arms. "We were young. We made mistakes."

Lewis pulled free of John, turned abruptly and walked up

the bank. He stopped and turned back. I could plainly see the tears running down his face and into his beard, even in the low light. "You forgot everything we swore on the eagle. We said we would die for each other." He stepped back toward John. "Not only did you leave us; you avoided us. You headed out to the Red River early ahead of your people so we couldn't find you, and when you came back, you shunned us. You broke Charles's heart."

John spread his arms. "I didn't think there was anything we could do that Chief Heckaton did not do. Crittenden gave him no other option, but to move down among the Caddo. I was bitter."

Lewis dropped his head. "You stupid Inyun."

John went up the bank and took Lewis's hand. "Lewis, there is never a night I close my eyes that I don't think on it. You are right. I broke the creed." He let go of Lewis's hand. "I have nothing left in the world now. I want to see *Khi-Dha' Zhu'te* again. I want to remember what it was like before."

Lewis didn't look up as John got into the pirogue and shoved us off.

John laid the paddle across the boat and turned to Lewis. "*A-Go-De.*"

Lewis looked up and raised his hand. "*Au revoir*, my friend, *au revoir.*"

Chapter 5

The river carried us along at a good clip. Going downriver is a pleasure, just hold the boat straight and let the river carry you. The sun was just rising when we saw big plumes of smoke to the south—steamboats. We agreed they were just below St. Charles long before we made it to St. Charles. We could tell there were more than three steamboats, but the smoke blended together and screwed up our count.

"I've never seen that many steamboats come up the river at the same time," I said. John said nothing and his face gave away nothing. "I heard the Yankees had taken Memphis, so there is nothing to keep them from coming on down the Mississippi and up the White," I said.

John watched the smoke, but remained silent as we neared St. Charles. Then I saw him looking toward the bank. There were a good many people walking upriver, looked like an exodus to me. I studied John's face, but it was iron. Not me—I was scared.

We came around the bend and there was St. Charles. Immediately I saw steamboats sunk in the river channel, pilot houses and stacks sticking out of the water. I saw the Mary Patterson right off. I knew her well. "What happened?" I said.

John pointed to pilings driven in a row across the river. "They tried to block the river and ran out of time, so they sunk these boats."

Then I noticed it. They had made a barricade across the river. I looked up on the bluffs; there were batteries of cannons up there, and farther down the river were more.

I pointed downriver. "That smoke is coming from Yankee gunboats." I turned to John. "They are going to fight right here!"

He kept paddling with the current.

"We have to turn around!"

He kept paddling and showed no fear or any other emotion.

"John, we have to turn around now!"

St. Charles sat on the high bluff banks on the right side of the river. John headed the boats toward the left side where there was nothing but woods. He pulled the boats to the bank. "You get behind these big cypress trees and don't move," he said.

"What are you going to do?" I said as I scurried behind the trees. Before he could answer, I looked up and saw the smoke downriver growing blacker. "They are building steam. They're fixin' to come up river. There is going to be a fight right here, John!"

I looked around to see him disappearing through the trees, walking downriver and toward the Yankees. I was too scared to stay by myself there, so I followed. He was not sneaking or creeping; he was marching toward something. Then I remembered: he was looking for the pecan tree with the double trunk. He was a fool.

As I followed, I could see the Confederate soldiers across the river. There were cannons everywhere—one great big gun on the highest bluff where the scuttled boats were, another big one just below that. There were other smaller guns farther downriver. One soldier yelled across the river at us.

My heart raced in my chest. I ran and caught John.

"I told you to stay back there behind those big cypress trees." He kept marching. I stayed right with him.

I could hear the men across the river yelling at each other to get ready. Orders were being given. I was more scared than I had ever been before—ever. If they started shooting, we were in the line of fire.

We could see the gunboats now. The steam engines on the boats roared louder and louder as the smoke billowed from the stacks; the very earth trembled. The front boat was a black, iron monster, looked like a giant, metal turtle with big pipes sticking out of its back, snorting smoke.

John stopped and I ran into his back. We were at the pecan tree with two trunks. He moved around to the back of it. I followed. He started digging with a small spade he had gotten from Lewis's place. He dug—I watched the gunboats getting closer. There was another black turtle and a wooden one, and others, but the smoke and steam was getting thick on the water and I was too scared to count them. They were beasts from the Lower Regions.

I looked around to see John pull a rotten piece of leather from the hole he had dug under the tree. He unwrapped it and pieces fell away revealing another piece of shell.

Suddenly an explosion rocked the very ground, then another and another. I looked up to see cannons firing from the riverbank on the other side. The gunboats answered with a deafening barrage. John and I both hit the ground. Pieces of flying debris showered all around us—wood, metal, and only God knows what else was flying through the sky.

John grabbed me and dragged me behind him as he ran. We dove over a fallen tree and buried down as close to the dirt as we could.

The explosions grew so loud that my ears hurt. Men were yelling, muskets sounded like firecrackers and the cannons belched pure hell.

"We need to get out of here!" I yelled at John as I started to get up.

He snatched me back down. "Too late. You will be cut to pieces."

He was right. We were only fifty yards from the edge of the river, and there was stuff flying everywhere. It sounded like woodpeckers working on the tree we were hiding behind, and there were queer whines as bullets ricocheted around us—made me think of a nest of yellow jackets. All at once, the big guns on the hills opened up. It must be close to what hell would be like. The ground shook and I whimpered like a frightened puppy. I wetted my pants. My ears hurt, felt like someone hitting them with a board when the big guns fired.

I lay with my head flat on the ground, but there was a hole under the log from which I could see. The lead black gunboat was directly in front of us. It rocked with the battle as its large guns fired. It crept forward, firing as it went. Bombs from the bluff guns bounced off its metal hull and tore through the trees over our heads like meteors, tearing the tops out of giant oaks.

Why didn't I stay back there behind those big cypress trees? If we live, I will never forgive this stupid Indian for getting us in such a spot.

I rolled over to see John bracing on his elbows, looking at the prize he had just dug up. He seemed not to care a damn about the war going on around us.

Suddenly a tree exploded overhead and large branches fell around us. John jumped on top of me to shield me from the falling limbs.

We huddled like that for a long time. Explosions, flying wood, and iron rained like hell. Smoke drifted through the trees, and the smell of spent gunpowder choked us.

I felt something on my hand; I looked to see a black snake crawling across it. I threw the snake and knocked John off me. I got to my knees and tried to compose myself as best I could. I trembled like I was freezing. The snake started back toward us and the log. I reckon he was afraid of all the commotion, too. John whacked it with the spade.

Upriver an explosion echoed across the water louder than the others. The sound was still ringing in my ears when I heard men screaming. I looked to see steam spewing from the lead gunboat, coming out of all holes and ports. The boat had been hit in a fatal spot and was drifting back downstream, spewing like a giant kettle.

John pulled me back down, so I quickly found my hole under the log where I could still see the action. Men were crawling out on the deck of the hit gunboat. They were screaming and withering on deck like worms thrown into hot coals—steam cooking sailors alive. The boat was slowly making its way downstream in front of us. Men from the crippled boat screamed for God and their mothers. Men from the bank yelled surrender or something. It was hard to tell.

The cannons across from us opened up on the boat as it drifted in front of them. Some of the men on the boat dove into the water. It was horrible. As the boat floated closer, I could see many of the men were scalded with skin hanging from them like wax from a candle. Blood and guts covered the deck, and the sailors were slipping and flopping in it like fish.

The Confederates came out of their entrenchments and

ran to the bank. They poured shot into the men on the deck and into the ones who had fallen or jumped into the river. Red floated in the water like paint as the shot men went down.

A sailor climbed up the bank in front of us. When he topped the bank, he saw our big log and started for it. When he was only a few feet from us, a red spot appeared on his chest, and he stopped and staggered like a drunk man. Above all the noise, I heard his last word: "Henry." He took a few more steps, then sank to the ground. I had a hard time catching my breath as the man twitched on the ground. His leg jerked one last time; then he moved no more.

The other gunboats moved up and began shelling the Rebel entrenchments. We heard musket fire farther behind their trenches. St. Charles was being surrounded by the Yankees.

John pulled me up, and we ran for the pirogues. Bullets whined and whirled around us. The woods looked very different than when we first walked through them—a cyclone couldn't have done more damage. I prayed as we ran, but kept saying the same words over and over: "Dear God— Dear God!" What else was there to say?

When we made it to the boats, John tied one behind the other. "What are you doing?" I said. I was scared and I wanted to go downstream away from this at top speed.

John said nothing. He grabbed a rope from the lead canoe and started pulling the boats. He looked like a train going through the woods.

I ran and grabbed his arm. "Where are you going?"

"We will drag the pirogues through the woods and around the battle and get back in the river," he said as he pulled loose from my grip and resumed dragging.

I stood there as he moved on. The battle was winding down. The shots were sporadic. The steam engines roared and whined. I could still hear men screaming. I just stood there and I wanted to go home. I didn't think about drawing birds. I didn't think about adventure. I thought about my momma and our safe farm. My pa was right and I was wrong.

I turned to see John moving through the woods. I followed. He didn't turn around. He knew I would come. I ran to him and grabbed his arm. "What are you doing?" I fell to my knees and began to sob. "I want to go home."

John turned to me. "We must get deeper in the woods. You are in danger here."

"What do you care?" I stood. "You brought us here! You are the one that put us in danger, you damn foolish Indian."

He said nothing, just looked straight into my eyes with no emotion. I lowered my head and looked at the ground. I wiped my nose on my sleeve and cried. "I saw that man die coming up the bank. I never seen a man die before." I couldn't stop sobbing. "All those men screaming on that boat." I looked up at him. "John, they were screaming for mercy, and those men shot them in cold blood."

The gunfire was tapering off from the battle. John looked through the woods as if he could see the battle beyond. "It is war. It has always been so." He shook his head. "*She'-Ga-He.*" He looked down and saw I didn't understand. "It means it is very bad."

I buried my face in his chest and sobbed. He stroked my hair. After a time, he said, "Come, let us go."

We pulled for about thirty minutes through cane thickets, then boggy sloughs under a forest of massive oaks cypress. The sound of battle had pretty much died away, but we could hear the deep song of the steam engines on the river at times. I grew tired and finally had to stop. "I have to rest. I can't go any farther for a while," I said.

John stopped and looked at me. He smiled. "*A-Goni.*" He flipped one of the pirogue's over. "It means 'sit.'" He motioned for me to sit on the bottom of the boat.

"Is that Quapaw talk?" I said as I dropped down on the boat.

He nodded and sat beside me.

I turned to him. "You speak French at times, too."

"*Oui.*"

"Sometimes my grandfather spoke French words," I said.

"My father and your grandfather were Frenchmen."

"Your mother was Quapaw?"

He nodded.

We said nothing for a long time. We both listened for the sounds of battle back toward the river. It was over. The gunboats were still at St. Charles, so that meant the Yankees had won. I worried for our farm. I wanted to go home. "Will the Yankees attack civilians?" I said.

He sat beside me on the boat. "No. They are only interested in fighting the Rebel Army. They will not bother your family. I do not believe they will get those big boats very far up the river. The water is too low."

I thought about that and agreed. It would be tough going.

After a short rest, we moved on and found a small lake in the woods. There was a well-used trail to it. It was obvious the trail led to St. Charles. There was a good campsite there, so we made camp and caught fish in the lake. As darkness settled around us, we cooked fish over the fire.

I watched John as he prepared the fire. I studied him as he cooked the fish. Everything he did was smooth and deliberate. He did remind me a lot of my grandfather. He softly sang some Indian song. I didn't understand any of the words, but it didn't matter; it was soothing to me, made me feel more comfortable on such a horrible day. The fire was small and inviting. I know why moths are drawn to fire; it is a lure. I sat there for the longest just looking into the flame, listening to the owls and crickets. I found myself humming along with John as he sang.

I didn't know this man before a few days ago. I had never heard of him. My folks may have talked about him, but I never put it together in my young mind. Yet, there I was sitting in camp with him like an old friend, like family.

I grabbed my tablet and began sketching the man and the fire. He knew what I was doing, but he continued singing and acting like I wasn't there. I studied the image hard, locked it in my mind so I could pull it back when I put the color to my art. It wasn't hard. The image would be in my head for the rest of my life. The day of battle would never leave me—not for one minute. Later in life I would paint the battle, but I couldn't bear to think on it then. I put the tablet away and turned to John. "This was not in my plans—this battle, this adventure."

John looked at me, then looked back at the fire.

"Where are we going? Why do you want me with you on this journey?" I said.

John said nothing as he poked at the fire.

"Well, then," I said, "I will go my own way at daylight."

John kept looking at the fire, but said, "We will be on the river long before daylight."

"What are you talk—"

"Get some sleep," he said. "We will move out in a couple of hours."

"I'm going my own way."

He turned toward me. "I need you, John. There is something I must show you. There is a purpose."

The fire danced in his brown eyes and shadows played on his weathered face. I had a strange feeling come over me. It was like I had been here before. I decided to trust the man. I wanted adventure—well, here it was. I got as comfortable as I could and tried to keep the thoughts of the battle from my mind. It was almost impossible, as it would be for the rest of my life. But, somehow, the crickets and crackling fire lulled me to sleep.

Chapter 6

When we put back into the river it was black-dark, around midnight. I could see the glow of campfires and lanterns back downriver toward St. Charles, the battle just a horrible memory. John pulled at the paddle harder than ever before. I couldn't match his stroke before—I sure couldn't now, but I gave it all I had. The moon, behind us, painted the river silver. It was waning now so it let the stars shine through, and their reflections were like little candles floating on the water.

The paddles swooshed as we dug into the river, but the pirogues lashed together so tightly made little sound. As I looked over at John, it was easy for me to think of a time when the Quapaw or Osage traveled this river, a time before white man, a time before steamboats and flatboats, a time when this world was theirs alone.

John seemed to focus on the horizon—what we could see of it with the moon's help. Occasionally he would scan the banks, but he seemed determined on what was just out of our sight down the river. I wondered what was on his mind. What did he know? What did he remember of this place? He had been gone a very long time. More than all that, what was he going to show me?

We went through a school of shad, and they skipped and danced on the water. The moon reflected off them, turning them into silver sparks. They bounced off the pirogues; some landed in the boats. It was like a magic show. John even smiled. That made me smile. It wasn't often he surrendered to emotion.

Farther down the river, we saw white waves crossing the river. We couldn't see the source, but the waves reflected like a streamer, spreading out into an ever increasing "V" shape. We paddled closer to discover three deer determined to cross the river, a doe and two fawns.

"Let us not get too close," John said. "They will try to climb in with us."

Their eyes were big and we could hear the heavy breathing and snorting. It reminded me of a horse running. I studied their features and stored them in my mind for another time when paint would meet canvas. We paddled beside them for a time; then we went our way.

"I bet you've killed a lot of deer in your day," I said.

John nodded. "I've killed many animals. They die so I live."

"You kill many bears?"

"Many *Wah-Saw*."

"That means bear in Quapaw?"

He nodded.

I said it several times, "*Wah-Saw*."

He smiled.

"Tell me the name for deer." I was eager to learn more.

"*Da*."

I repeated it.

"Fish?"

He pointed to one of the dead shad in the bottom of the boat. "*Hu.*"

"How do you say 'hello'?"

He waved with his hand. "*Ha-Wei.*"

"*Ha-Wei,*" I repeated several times.

He nodded his approval. "*U-Dah*: Good."

"*U-Dah.*"

He smiled again. "You would make a good Quapaw."

"What is *Khi-Dha' Zhu'te?*"

The smile left his face.

"You and Lewis talked about it back at his place."

He looked back ahead and began paddling.

I believed I had said something that he didn't want to talk about.

He suddenly stopped paddling and turned toward me. "It means 'red eagle.'" He looked off into the darkness for a time, then looked back at me, but said nothing.

"What did Lewis mean when he said he hoped you found it?"

John dug in hard with the paddle, and the pirogues shot through the water. "We will talk on it another time."

I knew that was the end of the conversation. I would ask him about it later. There were a good many things I would ask him later.

***

The dawn was growing, turning the river pink, and I was exhausted when John headed the boats to the southern shore.

"We will hide the boats here and go across the prairie by foot," John said as the pirogues slid upon the sand.

"I want to go into the Mississippi, then back up the Arkansas," I said.

He climbed from the boat. "Later."

We pulled the boats up the bank and covered them well with branches. John tied the boats to the trees very securely. I knew this was to keep high-water from taking them. He was not planning for us to come back soon.

We traveled through the thick timber not saying much to each other. He knew where he was going, but my plans had been altered beyond any recognition. I had dreamed of hitting the Mississippi and traveling back up the Arkansas. Now I was following this Indian, this half-breed, to I knew not where, nor why.

We walked for a long time, and I grew tired, but I just kept putting one foot in front of the other. I was not going to show weakness. I did not know why I wanted to impress this man, but I did.

I looked up ahead; he had stopped. He was sniffing the air again. I tried it, but smelled nothing other than the woods. Suddenly a dog began barking. It scared the mess out of me. I moved behind John.

He turned. "There is a house on the edge of the prairie up ahead. It was not there before."

"John, you have not been here in over thirty years," I said.

He surrendered a smile. "You are right, Little John; I will find more and more new surprises on this journey." He squeezed my shoulder. "The dog will not let us pass, so we will go to the dog."

He was right. The dog was soon upon us as we walked toward the house. The animal was the ugliest dog I had ever seen. He had so many colors that he looked like a patched quilt and shaggier than an old buffalo. He ran up to us and began licking us all over. He was also the most likable dog I had ever met.

The house was a small log cabin, and on the porch stood the owner, a man with very little hair, just a little ring around his head, above his ears. As we got closer, I could see he was smiling and had no teeth.

"What a dog you are, Jackson," he yelled. "You are bound to let them get me."

John held his hand up in a greeting manner as we walked toward the porch. I raised mine too. The dog licked the other.

The man sat down in a rocking chair he had there. "Come on up. If you are inclined to do me harm, there is nothing I can do about it."

We walked to the porch, and the man looked John up and down. "What brand Indian are you? Wait, don't tell." He rubbed his scraggly beard. "Not Cherokee, not Choctaw." He snapped his fingers. "Quapaw!"

John nodded. "*Hoo-Tah-Hey*."

He pointed at John. "That means 'real good.'"

John nodded again.

The man laughed. "Well, I be blamed. I just pulled that out of my a—" He looked at me and cut it off. "Young man, you are not an Indian."

"No sir."

No one said anything for a long spell. The dog jumped up on the porch and licked the man's hand.

"General Jackson, you are worthless." The man stood, then reached his hand down to us. "I'm Mr. Stilman." He shook John's hand, then mine, as we told him our names.

"Would you fellows like a nice, hot cup of coffee?" he said with a toothless smile.

"*Oui*," John said.

I said, "Oh, yessir; that would be first rate."

He slapped his leg. "Do you have any?" He bellowed like a jackass.

I laughed at him and with him. The dog did circles on the porch. John smiled and nodded.

He motioned for us to come into the cabin. "I tell you what, boys; I have some fresh cuttings from sassafras. We can have a brew from that. I have fresh honey, too. I've got the sting bumps to prove the freshness."

We set our stuff on the porch and went in with him. The cabin was even smaller on the inside. He had a homemade table and benches. There was a small bed along the wall and little else. The cabin reminded me of Lewis's place.

"Have a seat," he said. He fumbled around in the fireplace and soon had a small fire licking his pot. "Where did you fellows extract yourselves from, and where are you injecting yourselves to?"

I didn't know, so I said nothing.

After a spell John said, "Arkansas Post."

"Ah, The Post of Arkansas," Mr. Stilman said as he retrieved a pipe from a shelf. He went to the fire, lit a small stick, then lit his pipe with several deep, sucking draws. He offered us a puff as he sat at the table with us. We declined. "You a Confederate soldier?" he said, pointing the pipe at John.

John shook his head.

"Well then, I don't see what business an Indian would have there. The last time I was that way, they were building a fort and other trappings of war."

I turned to John to see his reaction—he was stony as ever.

Mr. Stilman leaned across the table and studied John. "I do declare there is more than Quapaw blood running through your veins." He leaned back, smiled, and took a deep draw from his pipe.

"The blood in me can lay claim to this very land your cabin sits on," John said evenly as he stood.

"Maybe long ago, but not any longer."

"I have proof," John said as dryly as ever.

Mr. Stilman choked a little as he exhaled the smoke. "Do tell. Do you have a deed?"

"What papers can an Indian have that a white man will

honor?"

Mr. Stilman grinned big. "Well now, Mr. Quapaw, without a legal deed, you have no claim to anything—white man's law."

John growled, "*Pe'-Zi.*" He turned and went out the door.

I don't know what the word meant, but he was clearly disgusted. I was surprised by the rare show of emotion.

He came back in with his bag, pulled out a rolled up paper, and threw it on the table.

Mr. Stilman looked at it, then up at John.

John motioned for him to read it.

Mr. Stilman bit down on the pipe with his lips, then reached and unrolled the paper. He mumbled across the pipe as he read. He slowly looked up and took the pipe from his lips. "Are you John R. Gillette?"

"*Oui.*"

Mr. Stilman dropped his pipe on the table and sank down on the bench.

I pulled the document to me, but I couldn't make heads or tails of it. "What does it mean?"

"It means this Quapaw owns all the land around here as far as you can see," Mr. Stilman said with a deep sigh.

John rolled the document back up and placed it back into his bag.

"How can an Indian own so much land?" Mr. Stilman said. "It can't be legal."

"We lived on this land long before white man came, but it's the white man's law and my white man's blood that says I own the land."

Mr. Stilman pulled away from the table and retrieved three tin cups from the shelf. He placed them on the table and poured the steaming brew from the pot. He put a bowl of honey on the table, too.

I pulled the cup to me. It smelled inviting. I spooned a

little of the honey into it. The others did the same. We were soon sipping, but saying nothing.

Mr. Stilman broke the silence. "John, is that document legal, sure nuff?"

"It is legal. Taxes and everything paid."

I turned to John. "How did you pay the taxes from Indian country?"

"It was arranged."

"Did you have that deed before you returned?" I said.

He didn't answer.

"You stole it from our house."

"I did not steal what is mine."

"How did you know where to get the deed from our house?" I demanded.

He stared at me. "We will talk on this another time."

I said nothing else on the matter.

Mr. Stilman was not listening to our bickering. He said, "I don't know where I will go. I'm too old to strike out again." He looked at us with longing eyes.

The dog noticed his owner and nuzzled his nose to the man's hand.

"General Jackson, it looks like we are out in the cold," Mr. Stilman said as he rubbed the dog's ear.

"How did you come to be here?" John said.

Mr. Stilman forced a smile. "I've been here a long time now, never knew for sure who possessed this land, but I did hear the name 'Gillette' tossed around. I figured no one cared about this spot in the woods." He patted the dog, then looked up at us. "I was in the army and attached to one of those private companies that moved the Creek Indians from Alabama. It was somewhere around 1836, I think. I can't remember."

"Moved them where?" I said.

"Out west close to where my tribe was sent," John said.

"That's right. You see, I served under General Jackson in the old days when I was young. I thought him a fine general, a fine man, and fine president. He was none of them. When I saw what those poor Indians went through, and for no good reason except to give the land to the white people, I changed my thinking. They had done everything the white people wanted. They had almost become like white folks, but they could never do enough. President Jackson made those people suffer."

"What happened to them?" I said.

"We marched them—Creek, Choctaw, Seminole, and Cherokee from the East all the way to the other side of Arkansas. Some went by land, some by water, some both. I was on a steamboat transporting Creeks. We came from Alabama to Rock Roe up on the White River."

"Rock Roe near Clarendon?" I said.

"Yes. The company worried about getting the Indians out fast and cheap. They cared little for the health of the Indians." He wiped his eyes. "I saw many a little child die on the trip. I saw many a mother cry. You can imagine thousands of people being driven from their homes—the only home they ever knew."

I looked at John, and he was staring at the wall.

"When we unloaded at Rock Roe, the company was supposed to have procured enough wagons for the trip across Arkansas. They had nowhere near enough for the hundreds of people, many women and children, that we had there on the banks of the White River. They would have to walk. They would be rushed, and I knew many would die." He began to cry. "I could not stand it, so I slipped away." He sobbed loudly. "I could not help the poor people so I ran away. This is where I ended up. I changed my name and hid right here in these woods below the prairie."

John said, "I see why you named your dog General

Jackson."

Mr. Stilman wiped his eyes and smiled. "Yeah, he is the most pitiful looking dog I ever saw." He rubbed the dog. "I love this pitiful dog, but I hope the other Jackson is in hell."

"*Oui*," John said.

Mr. Stilman looked at John. "I know about your people. It was just as bad, if not worse. I met a Quapaw once over on the Arkansas that stayed behind."

John stood. "Mr. Stilman, I do not want your cabin. You can stay here as long as you wish."

"Thank you." Mr. Stilman blubbered and bent down and squeezed his dog.

The more I learned about John, the more I liked him.

***

That night I lay on an old buffalo robe. It smelled like the buffalo was still wearing it, but that animal had been dead for generations. John was asleep on the floor across from me, and Mr. Stilman, in his bed, was mumbling in his sleep. I listened to the barred owls scream and holler. Somewhere in the distance I could hear a lone great-horned owl softly hoot. I thought about the Quapaw. They had lived on these very grounds for hundreds of years, maybe thousands, maybe more, and now they are gone. I looked up at Mr. Stilman, and thought of him as a young man torn between his duty as a soldier and what was morally right, living here in this lonely place hiding from his past and fighting his demons.

The moonlight shown through the only window, bathing the inside of the cabin with a bluish glow. A mouse ran across the floor and climbed up on the bed with Mr. Stilman. I'm sure he will visit me and my buffalo robe before the night is over. General Jackson, lying on the front porch, started scratching, and it sounded like somebody hammering on the porch. I was grateful the itch wasn't severe.

Before I could fall asleep, a fear was realized. I saw that

sailor at St. Charles running towards us and being shot. I tried not to think about it, but it was no good. I could see his wet hair. I could see the fear on his scalded face, the skin hanging, pink and red. I heard his last word over and over: "Henry...Henry...Henry." I tried to block it from my mind, but it was no use. "Henry." Who was Henry, a brother, cousin, friend? The cannons fired in my head. The men screamed on the steaming gunboat. The man's last word: "Henry...Henry."

I climbed up from the robe and went out the door. General Jackson met me with a lick on the hand. The cool night air was refreshing, but it didn't erase the soldier's scalded face from my mind. I sat in the rocking chair and wept. I just wanted to go home now. I just wanted to go home.

A lone wolf howled in the distance. His song was haunting and long. General Jackson gave a muffled bark, then curled back up on the porch; he had heard it too many times before.

"He's out on the prairie," John said. "They like to hunt in the tall grass."

I hadn't heard him come out, and it startled me a little.

He put his hand on my shoulder. "The prairie starts beyond those trees." He pointed toward the north. "Our prairie."

"There is a prairie behind our house," I said.

He looked down at me. "It is all the same. It's broken up with sloughs and creeks and forests here and there, but it is all the same prairie." He patted my head and walked to the edge of the porch and stared off into the distance. "My grandfather talked of great herds of buffalo on that prairie— antelope, too. My people hunted them right there on that very prairie beyond those trees." He said nothing for a long time. Finally, he said, "Only white man's cattle graze the tall grass now."

"Did you hunt the prairie?"

"Our villages were on the south side of the Arkansas River, but I stayed on the prairie. Your grandfather hunted with me." He looked down at me, smiled. "He thought he was Quapaw, too."

"Where did your father live? Did he live in the Quapaw village?"

He laughed. "No. My father lived at Arkansas Post, but he traveled all over. He was a wealthy man, owned a store at the post."

"Your mother was Quapaw. Did she like living at the Post?"

He took a deep breath. "She went back to her people, and I went with her. Father was a good man, and he was good to the Quapaw, but he was always in the wind going somewhere. We were at home with the people."

"What happened to your people? Why did they leave?"

John said nothing for a long time. The wolf howled again. John smiled at the wolf, then said, "My people were good to the French, and they were good to my people, but my people depended on them too much after a while. They depended on white man things and white man ways. We were once a great nation." He looked down at me. "My grandfather told me stories how we fought the Chickasaw and the Choctaw and Osage to protect the French. Our lands ranged clear to the other side of the Mississippi, north to the mountains, out west for hundreds and hundreds of miles, and south to the Caddo people."

"Our farm near DeValls Bluff was Quapaw land?" I said.

"Yes."

"I didn't know that."

"When the French left, the Spanish came. They were not good like the French. After them, came the Americans—the worst. They took and took and took. By the time I was born, we were not so strong anymore, not so many. In 1818 Chief Heckington gave up all of our land north of the Arkansas to the Americans, including the great prairie."

"Why?"

"I reckon he thought they would leave us alone. They promised money and goods, but they didn't keep their end of the deal. The Americans kept coming, and in 1824, he gave up more. We were finally driven from our lands and were sent south to live among the Caddo. They didn't want the Quapaw either. Floods washed our crops away down there, and many of my people died, including my first wife. We trickled back into Arkansas. In the 1830s the Quapaw were finally sent to the Indian Territory out west. My people are there now, but scattered, some with other tribes."

"That is truly a sad story," I said. "Why didn't you and your mother stay with your father?"

He took a deep breath. "He died before my people were driven from our land."

"But you have all this land. You could bring your people here."

He laughed. "I own this land because I am half white, not because I am half Indian. The second it was found out that the Quapaw were coming back, they would take the land."

I knew he was right.

"They have pushed most Indians west. The Indians in the far west will not have their country for long. The Americans will not be satisfied until they have everything between the oceans."

I lowered my head. I was an American. He was talking about my people, and I felt a guilt come over me like a thundercloud.

He squeezed my shoulder. "You must not feel bad. You did nothing to the Quapaw."

"I am an American, and it was my people that were and

are bad to the Indians."

"John Gillette, you are part French and they were good to my people. I am half white, so do I blame myself?"

I wiped my eyes and looked at him, but I didn't know what to say.

"The Chickasaw, Choctaw and Osage killed my people. Do I blame them? The Caddo didn't want my people. Do I blame them? There were tribes in the West that were not good to us. Do I blame them?"

"Who is to blame?" I said.

"I think on this often. I can never come to an answer. Maybe if the white man had never come to America it would have been a good thing." He took a deep breath. "Sooner or later it was going to happen. The Indians pushed out weaker Indians, and the white man pushed out all of the Indians. Man is a mean creature."

We looked up to see a shooting star stream across the heavens.

"Someday maybe another race will push out the white man. Who will be the blame, then?"

I thought about what he had said. I could never come up with an answer as who to blame. I still can't, but as a white, I have always felt guilty.

"Come, John; let us get some sleep," John said as he helped me from the chair.

The mouse leaped from the table as we went in.

***

I was awakened by a chopping sound coming from outside. I was the only soul in the cabin. I went outside to relieve myself and found John whacking on a long stick.

"What are you making from that bean pole?"

John looked away from his work. "Stilman had this hickory pole stored away on the porch here, said he was going to use it to hang deer. He let me have it."

I went behind the cabin and took care of my business. When I returned, John was drawing the knife down the stick, shaving off layers of wood.

"What are you making?" I said.

"A bow."

I sat on the porch and watched him work. He pulled the knife down the stick, then he would bend it, then he would do the same to the other side. He would shave more wood until he had the bow bending evenly on both ends.

"Starting to resemble a bow now," I said, "but it has a hump on it."

He rubbed the hump. "It is a knot. If I cut it out, my bow will be weak there. I have to leave it. The knot makes it my bow." He smiled.

He shaved and carved until he was satisfied. He handed me the bow to examine while he started a fire with a pile of sticks he had collected.

"What are you doing with the fire?" I said.

He took the bow back, cut notches on each end to hold the string, and didn't answer about the fire, just kept whittling and carving. He looked over and sighted down it. "See that curve in the bow?" he said, letting me look down it.

"Yeah, it sort of rolls away from center on one end."

He held the bow over the fire and moved it around. I could see he was trying to get it hot without getting it black or catching it afire. He pulled the bow out of the fire and bent it over the porch rail. He held it there for about five minutes, then sighted down the bow. He handed it to me. "Don't touch the hot part."

I took the bow and looked down it. It was almost straight now. "Well, I'll be darn."

He took the bow back and put it over the fire again. This time he went through the same procedure and straightened it almost perfectly. He smiled and nodded.

He went to the porch and retrieved something from his bag. It was a string. After fiddling with it for a bit he fitted it to the bow. It was so long it barely curved the bow. He placed the center of the string over a nail on the porch and pulled down on the bow.

"What are you doing now?" I said.

Still pulling, he said, "I'm seeing which side of the bow is bending the most and shaving a little more wood from the side that is the stiffest. I want the limbs to bend the same." He took the bow down and shaved a little wood away with his knife. He put it back on the nail and did this a few more times until he was satisfied with the bow. Then he shortened the string and fastened it to the bow. Now it looked like a bow. He pulled on it a few times and nodded.

I touched the string. "What is this made of?"

"I made it from sinew, tendons from deer. I can make a bow from anything, and it doesn't take too long, but the string takes longer. I make them whenever I come across tendon. I save them for when I need them."

"A bow is too big to carry on a long journey, but you just tucked that string away in your bag," I said.

Mr. Stilman came from a little shed around back. He had a bundle of short river cane in his hands. "Here." He handed it to John.

John smiled. "Just the right size."

"I use that small cane to make rabbit traps and such, but I have plenty," Mr. Stilman said.

John nodded. "Good and dry, too." He sighted down one and took it to the fire. He rolled it in the flame, took it out and bent it over his knee.

"What are you doing?" I said. "Just right for what?"

He sighted down it again, then repeated the process. He looked at me while he was rolling the arrow in the fire. "These small canes make good arrows. I'm straightening them like I did with the bow."

"Got a couple turkey wings in the shed, too," Mr. Stilman said. "Killed a big ole gobbler last month."

"*Merci*," John said.

Mr. Stilman smiled and nodded.

John reached into his bag again. This time he came out with pretty arrowheads.

"You make those?" I said.

"What kind of an Indian would I be if I couldn't make my own arrows?"

"A starved one," Mr. Stilman said. Mr. Stilman and I laughed.

It didn't take John long to fashion a few arrows, and I only wish I could shoot a rifle as well as he could shoot that hickory bow. He shot the bow all day. He tried to teach me, but I was a hardheaded learner. He shot five squirrels from a mulberry tree. Mr. Stilman cleaned them for our supper.

***

The next morning we were up before daylight. Mr. Stilman made us more brew of his sassafras tea—I came to like the stuff. We finished off the squirrel stew left from the night before, along with biscuits that were flatter than a shingle.

As we were eating, I noticed that Mr. Stilman was quieter than he had been. He would look at John, rub his bald head, and look away. He did this quite a few times. After a while John had enough. John dropped his fork with a clang and looked at Mr. Stilman. "*Tah'-Tah!*"

It startled Mr. Stilman and me.

"I-I-I don't know what that means." Mr. Stilman said.

John softened. "It means 'what.' You keep looking at me; you want to tell me something."

Mr. Stilman put his hands on the table, palms down. He looked at them for a time, then looked up at John. "I'm sorry for what the white man has done to your people."

"I've told you I'm not going to make you leave."

"That has nothing to do with it." Mr. Stilman raised his hands and slowly rubbed them together. "I've seen too much suffering." He began to tear. "As a white man, I feel responsible."

John rose from the table. "We must go now."

I was suddenly furious. Here was a man with his heart breaking, and John lets him suffer. But I dutifully got my bag and followed John out the door.

As we stepped off the porch, General Jackson was running in circles in the yard. I reached down and rubbed his ears. John grabbed up his bow and quiver and started across the yard.

Mr. Stilman stepped out onto the porch and called after us, "I welcome you to come back by any time."

John turned. "Mr. Stilman, do not blame yourself for what has happened to the Indians. If a pack of wild dogs attacked you, and General Jackson tried to protect you, would you kill him along with the wild dogs simply because he, too, was a dog?"

Mr. Stilman wiped his eyes, smiled and raised his hand.

John raised his. "*Au revoir.*"

Mr. Stilman returned, "Good-bye."

I followed John as we heard Mr. Stilman calling to General Jackson.

Chapter 7

The prairie spread out before us like a sea of grass. Small birds fluttered and darted around the tops of the tall grass, chasing bugs. Little indigo buntings rode the tops of the grass stalks eating the seed tops. John looked at me and smiled. I smiled back. The grass was tall—in places, taller than a man. We waded into it following a deer trail. The trail was alive with mice, lizards, and all kinds of little animals.

I followed John down the trail as one deer might follow another. He ran his hands across the grass as we walked, stopped to study a mantis eating a grasshopper. He would often pause to sniff the wind, smiling when he would pick up something pleasant in the breeze. I'm sure he was remembering the old days. I said nothing, tried to lay back and let him remember the past. I didn't want to be an intruder on his memories.

We soon struck a road and started north, and John's

demeanor changed as surely as a rain cloud spoils a sunny day. The road brought him back to the now. He was sure the road went from Arkansas Post to St. Charles, but the road had not been there years ago. We followed that road for a time until we came to woods and a creek. Then we left the road and followed the creek. John was soon in high feather again—things were once again, if only for a short spell, as they were in the old days. We walked for miles, jumping deer and all sorts of wild critters.

"These creeks and woods cut all through and around the big prairies," John said. "There is plenty of game here."

I pitched down by a gum tree. "How far to whatever we are searching for?"

John stopped and looked down at me. "We will be there by dark. But you have to keep going."

"Let's rest a spell."

He sat down beside me as softly as a bird sits a nest.

"Have you ever been to this very spot before?" I said.

He looked around and smiled. "I have followed this creek many, many times. The four of us—your grandfather, Lewis, Paul, and me roamed this area like a pack of wolves. We hunted and fished and just lived life to the top."

I smiled thinking about it. "How old were you?"

"Me and Charles prowled the prairie when we were just boys, twelve, maybe. We met Lewis and Paul a little later. I don't remember how we became such friends, but by the time we were in our twenties—young men, we were together all the time."

I leaned against the tree thinking about the four of them. I'm sure they were a strange group: an Indian, Frenchman, Negro, and American.

"Up. We must move on," he said and rose without touching the ground with his hands.

We walked for miles, me way behind. Suddenly he

stopped, drew his bow, and shot. I saw a prairie chicken take to the wing, and John shot again. The bird went to the ground in a feathery ball. I had not even seen John string another arrow before the second shot was off.

I ran to him. "What a good shot! You missed the first shot, but you got him on the second."

John handed me the chicken with the arrow sticking out both sides. I admired the bird. He went over to where he first shot and picked up another chicken.

"Two! You killed two!"

John grinned. "*Oui*. You have to eat also."

We gutted the birds and continued on. As I followed the Indian, I reflected on how fast he had shot and how easily he had killed the birds, no aiming, no guessing where to put the arrow, no thinking about it at all. He just shot, then shot again. I always wondered how the old Indians lived off the land. I never wondered after that day.

Everything was simple with John. He made the bow from a stick. He had made the strings from tendons of a deer. The arrows were fashioned from river cane and turkey feathers. He had made the points from rocks. The quiver was from a beaver hide that Mr. Stilman had stretched on a board. Everything was made from things in nature, and he killed the birds as dead as with a shotgun. The only weapon on him not of nature was his knife.

John stopped and motioned for me to come up. He pointed toward the creek. I followed the direction to where he was pointing in the water. There was a big bullfrog just on the edge of the water about ten yards away.

He pulled a cane arrow from his quiver. It had no arrowhead on it, just a blackened stick stuck into the end of the cane. He placed the arrow onto the bowstring and handed the bow to me.

"Look at the frog, nothing else," he said. "Don't think

about the arrow or the bow; just think only of the frog. Pull the bow back until the string touches your face, then hold still, only think of the frog. Find a small spot on that frog, all your attention there."

I took the bow. "When do I release the string?"

"Do not think about the string, only the spot on the frog. When you come to full draw, become solid and still as a tree, think of where the arrow will enter the skin on the frog. Think of that spot, nothing else. Don't think of hitting or missing, only the arrow going into that spot."

I gripped the bow. It felt good, so light, but I now knew its power.

"Only the frog," John whispered.

I stared at the frog. I found a black spot about the middle and looked only at the spot; it moved up and down with the frogs breathing. I knew I was drawing the bow, but I was thinking of the spot. There was a small piece of duckweed stuck to the spot, so I concentrated on it. Somewhere in the back of my mind I felt the string touch my face, but I paid it no mind—only the spot on the frog. I never saw the arrow. I never looked for the arrow. I stared at the spot just as John instructed me. My body was stiff, firm as the side of a barn. I could not see the whole frog, only the spot. Suddenly the frog jerked. The arrow was buried into his head, and he was pinned to the muddy bank. I did not remember shooting. I did not tell myself to release the string, but my arrow was in the frog. I did not hit the small piece of duckweed, but I did hit the frog.

John patted me on the back. "Now you know the spirit of the arrow, the magic of the bow."

I looked down at the hickory bow in my hand. I saw the grain of the wood, the fray of the sinew, the tool marks where John had worked the wood, the big knot in the wood, and I did see the magic. I looked back at the cane arrow shaking from the quivering frog. By that point I had killed many animals with a gun or trap. This was different! It must be what a hawk feels when he catches a pigeon, what a wolf feels when he takes down a deer, not like killing with a gun. I felt like a real predator—like a wolf.

I fetched the frog and brought it back dangling from the end of the arrow. I was so proud I almost teared up.

John pulled the dead frog from the arrow. He shook it. "We will kill more, and feast on prairie chickens and bullfrogs."

We did take more. I missed more than I hit, but we had plenty for supper.

We walked away from the creek and woods and came out on a savannah. The sun was very low so we made camp next to the prairie. I gathered wood for a fire while John carved on a flat piece of wood.

"What are you doing?" I said.

John looked up from his work. "Come see."

John had taken a flat piece of wood and carved a small bowl-shape into it, about an inch around. Then he cut a V-shape from the edge of the wood into the depression. He placed the board down onto a pile of grass—it looked like a bird nest. He stuck a stick into the bowl-shape. The stick was about two feet long. He placed the top of the stick between his hands and began rubbing his hands together, causing the stick to go back and forth quickly. Soon smoke drifted from the bowl. He rubbed faster and the smoke grew stronger. Suddenly a small ember rolled out of the V-shape onto the bird nest. John bent down and blew until the bird nest erupted into flame. He scooped the nest up and put it under our firewood.

As the fire grew, I said, "You made that look easy."

John placed dried grass over the flame to help it grow. "It is not hard—it is not easy. It is necessary."

"You can get everything you need from the land, can't you?"

John stood up from the fire and looked into my eyes. "We would be better off if we all did that. White man wastes so much—too much—to have so little. We could use only little to save so much."

I looked at John's bow leaning on a bush. I thought about what it took to make that bow as opposed to what it takes to make a gun. Just the firewood alone to fire the steel would be a thousand times more than the wood to make the bow.

***

The sun sank below the bushes and prairie grass, and doves flew across the orange sky. The frogs and chickens cooked slowly over the small fire as John hummed his Indian song. I nibbled on blackberries we had just picked at the edge of our camp. We both sat close to the fire to keep the mosquitoes away.

I'm not sure what John was thinking, but I was thinking about what he had told be earlier. He had grinned when I said the world would be better if we only lived wild like the Indians. He had told me the Indians had large fields, and burned the trees and prairies for their own use, dug ditches, damned streams, built great mounds. He said Indians were no more wild than the Europeans—maybe not as wild. He said the Indians just didn't waste so much and appeared to be more tied to Mother Earth. He had looked at me and said, "People are people; some good, some not so good."

John pulled one of the frogs from the stick and declared it done. He retrieved salt from his bag and sprinkled it on the meat, and we went to work. The prairie chickens were the best I'd ever had, but the frogs were a little dry—still delicious, but a little dry.

I threw the frog bones into the fire and grabbed another from the stick. My mind would not let go of what the prairie must have been like before white man. I looked at John eating his frog and wondered if he was thinking the same.

Before I could say anything, John pointed along the edge of the prairie to a treeline. "You see that tall tree there, the one taller than the rest?"

With the low light, I could see the silhouette of a lone cypress tree, much taller than the others. "I see it."

"Your grandfather Charles climbed that tree almost to the top." He turned to me and smiled.

"How did he get up there?"

"The tree is too big at the bottom, but there was another tree that was smaller and leaned into the big tree. He climbed it, then got over into that tree."

"Why? That old tree is over a hundred feet tall."

John laughed, stood and walked over to me. He sat down beside me and crossed his legs. "Lewis dared him."

I shook my head. "That's all it took?"

"We were about your age, sixteen or seventeen; we did foolish things. We ran wild like deer across the prairie, the four of us. We would meet up and stay gone in the wild for days. Your grandfather and me would always be in trouble when we got back home, but Paul and Lewis—well, they really had no family that cared. Lewis lived with his father in camps all along the rivers. Paul lived around the Post. I never knew where he came from. He had no family, and if he was a slave, his owner didn't care where he went or what he did. He was a strange character, could speak French, Spanish, Quapaw, and Cherokee. Looking back down the years, I believed he was a slave to the Cherokee when they came to Arkansas, but somehow got away or was let loose or something."

"I bet y'all had many adventures."

"Indeed, we did. We all made ourselves buckskins and lived off the land. My grandfather told us of the old days, and we tried to relive those old days." John said. "We were an odd bunch of Quapaws." He looked into the now darkness, smiled and reflected.

"How did Grandfather get down from that tree?" I said.

The smile left his face. He took a deep breath and looked at me. He ran his fingers across his graying hair. "I told you there is something I wanted to show you. Remember?"

"I remember."

He leaned over and threw a couple of pieces of wood on the fire. The old wolf yelped down near the creek.

"John Gillette, listen to my story very carefully. Only me and Lewis are alive to remember. No one else knows. You are Charles's grandson, and you are much like him. You will be the last of us." John began his story.

***

We saw Charles looking at something across the prairie; he could see for miles up there. We yelled up at him, and he told us to be quiet. Satisfied at what he had seen, he came down that tree like a bear cub. To this day it's hard to believe how fast he came down that tree.

He jumped the final ten feet to the ground and motioned us to him. We could see right off something was terribly wrong.

"Osage coming down the prairie," he said.

"What?" Lewis said.

"Are you sure?" I said.

"About ten or so on horseback."

"Probably Cherokee," Lewis said.

"I don't think so," Charles said. "They are a far piece, but I don't think so."

"What are they doing this far south on the prairie?" Paul said.

"Revenge." I said.

Charles spread his hands, questioning.

I rubbed my head and kicked at a weed. "The Cherokee attacked the Osage about two months ago. I heard the elders say they will come for revenge against the Quapaw."

"That's plumb crazy," Lewis said. "The Cherokee attacked them, not the Quapaw."

"The Elder's say the Osage consider the Cherokee invaders to this side of the Mississippi. The Osage believe we should side with them and not the Cherokee. The Elders have been expecting something since the attack."

"Aw, bear turds. I don't believe none of it," Lewis said. "They would have to ride right through Cherokee territory to get here."

"That is why there are so few. They will hit quick and escape. They will want to leave a message to us 'traitors.'"

"We have to warn the people," Paul said.

"There is no time," Charles said. "They will be there before us."

"Then we have to stop them," I said.

Lewis shoved me. "That's half-breed nonsense."

"He's right," Paul said. "They could even attack the Post."

We all looked to Charles. He was always the smart one of the bunch. He looked toward the low sun, then back toward the prairie. "It's getting late," Charles said. "They will stop where the road crosses the creek. They will water their horses and wait there for darkness."

Lewis threw his hands in the air. "How in the world do you know what they're gonna to do? First, you can tell they are Osage from a mile away. Second, you can read their minds."

"Shut your mouth, Lewis," Paul said. "Because you are big and dumb, don't blame us."

"Charles is right," I said. "If they are Osage, they will wait until dark. The creek crossing would be the smartest place to wait; there they can water their horses and hide in the trees."

"You would agree with your cousin if he said they were pink Indians riding turtles," Lewis said.

We all looked at Lewis, but said nothing.

Lewis picked his bow up from the ground. "Well then, what is the plan?"

I pulled one of my arrows from my quiver and drew the road and the creek crossing in the dirt. "I believe they are aiming to hit the Post since they are so far down the prairie. They will target the Quapaws's camped around the Post—much easier and safer than attacking the Quapaw villages."

"I believe you are right," Charles said.

"Makes sense," Paul said.

Lewis said nothing, but he was studying my map.

I resumed. "We need to get between them and the Post. All we have to do is make a little fuss, and when they find they are discovered, they will race back up the prairie."

Suddenly there was a rumbling to the west. We looked that way to see the flash of lightning.

"Well, let's light a shuck if we are going to get there in time," Lewis said.

We grabbed our bags and bows and headed to the crossing. I felt an emotion in me I had never felt before. My people were once many and a proud, a strong nation. Now we were few and not the warriors we once had been. But now here I was, an *O-Gah-Pah*, about to attack our old enemy, the Osage. I felt a tingling all through my body as we raced through the prairie.

                              ***

We stopped short of the crossing and made our plans. Charles and I would cross the road while Lewis and Paul stayed on this side. I would give the signal with a bird call. We yell, shoot one arrow, then high-tail it back to the big cypress tree. We figured it would be enough to turn the small band. They would figure they had been discovered and their sneak attack would not work.

We crawled to the road. I could see their horses drinking water from the creek, but I didn't see the men. I had an uneasy feeling. Charles and I crawled to the other side of the road.

Quicker than I can tell you this, we were suddenly surrounded. They appeared out of the tall grass like vapors. Charles was right; they were Osage, and now they had guns leveled at all our heads. We should have known better. They were the best warriors the Osage had, and we were young fools.

They took our weapons and one grabbed me up from the ground. He was big, but he was a white man. He was an Indian now, but he was white. He yelled at me in his language. It was close to our language, and I made out *O-Gah-Pah* dog.

"Speak English so we can understand you, you red heathen!" Lewis yelled as they gathered us together. The Osage closest to him backhanded him.

The "white" Osage made a sign with his hand, and this kept the other Osage from hitting Lewis again.

We found there were only ten of them as they shoved the four of us together. They talked among themselves. They were still going to attack the Post.

The white one shoved me. "You not smart attack us; only pups."

"Why do the great Osage warriors come here to attack?" Charles said.

He turned to Charles. "*O-Gah-Pah* coward, *oui*. Cherokee come; take land from *O-Gah-Pah* and *Wa-Zha-Zhe* "*O-Gah-Pah* not fight Cherokee. Cherokee kill many *Wa-Zha-Zhe* because *O-Gah-Pah* cowards."

"Osage kill everybody, including a good many Cherokee," Lewis said. "Besides, you're not Osage—you're as white as I am."

He grabbed Lewis by his collar. He hit his own chest with his other hand and said, "*Wa-Zha-Zhe*! *Wa-Zha-Zhe*!"

"Lewis, shut your mouth," Paul said.

Suddenly lightning flashed and thunder cracked like a whip.

The white one made a motion with his hand, and they pushed us before them back toward the creek and their horses.

Charles and I walked beside each other. Lewis and Paul were behind us.

"Think they will kill us?" Charles said.

"They will kill us." I had no doubt of it.

It was growing late, but it was even more dark because of the building storm clouds. The lightning was striking all around, and I could see the concern in some of the Osage warriors' eyes. The trees began to fan and whip with the brewing winds.

When we got to the horses, the warriors talked among themselves. I heard enough to know they were getting ready to kill us. They walked us away from the road. I knew they didn't want our bodies discovered.

I whispered to Charles. "When I run, you run. I'm sure Lewis and Paul will do the same."

"Right," Charles said. "It's the only way."

About fifty yards from the road, they stopped us. I knew what was coming.

"Run!" I yelled.

I turned to run back past the Osage, hoping they couldn't get their guns up in time to get a clean shot. When I turned, I knocked one down. I saw one had his gun trained at Paul. There was no way Paul could escape. I ran between Paul and the gun.

Suddenly everything flashed bright white and blue. Fingers

of lightning bolts flew in all directions like a tangled spiderweb. The sound was like a thousand guns shot at once. Limbs and leaves and splinters flew in all directions. I was either thrown to the ground or dove to the ground—it all happened in an instant. Everything went dark and I could hear nothing.

Slowly my senses came back to me. As I rose, only Paul was standing, and he was staggering and covering his eyes. Charles got to his knees, then Lewis. I counted nine of the Osage—they did not move.

Smoke rose in little curls from the bodies and body parts. There was a smell in the air like meat cooked over a fire.

I heard moaning and turned to see the white Osage. He was cut in half, but he was still alive. I got up and stood over him. Charles, Lewis, and Paul walked up, too. No one said anything as the man lay their moaning. Suddenly the wind stopped and there was an eerie quiet except for the moans.

The man whispered words, but I couldn't understand. Charles got closer, but shook his head when he didn't understand, either.

Something came over me and I picked the man's knife from the ground beside him. I showed the man the knife. "I am *O-Gah-Pah*." I grabbed his ponytail up until his neck was stretched. He made a gurgling sound. I carved a gash in his scalp, but Charles knocked the knife from my hand.

"I won't stand for you to scalp him," Charles said. "You are not a savage."

I found one of the Osages' guns on the ground and shot the man to put him out of his misery.

We looked at each other not knowing what to say. We were just seconds from death, and now we were standing over our enemy and they were all dead.

Lewis broke the silence. "Look!"

We turned to see him pointing at a big oak beside the

creek. Part of the top was blown out by the lightning, smoke still rising from the tree. The lightning had run down the trunk and knocked a hole from the bottom. There were shiny objects scattered on the ground before the tree.

"What the hell?" Lewis said.

Charles went over and picked up a piece. He turned. "This is shell from the ocean."

We gathered three pieces. They had carvings on them, birds and swirls. They were Indian pieces, but they weren't Quapaw—least ways, nothing that I was familiar with. The three pieces fit together, but there was still a hole where one or more fit.

"Looks like they came out of the tree," Paul said as he picked up another piece at the base. This completed the puzzle; it was a perfect seashell.

Charles examined the tree. "This old tree could be hundreds of years old." He pointed to the base of it. "Look! There is a hole about a foot from the ground. I bet this stuff was in there. When the lightning hit the tree, it blew this stuff out of it."

Lewis bent down at a tuft of grass. "Lookie here." He picked up a red object and turned it over in his hands.

We all went to inspect it.

"It's a redbird," Paul said.

Charles took it. "It's an eagle." He held it up to get a better look. "It's about as perfect as it gets."

It was, indeed, a carving of an eagle. It was a yellowish-red stone, but you could almost see through it. It was a perfect carving, down to the feathers.

"I wager that is made outta a big ruby," Lewis said.

"There is something in it," Paul said, pointing to the middle of the stone.

The storm had passed and the sun shown behind the clouds as it started down below the trees. Charles held the bird up toward the sun. We gathered in close to look. There was a small creature embedded in the red stone. It resembled some type of lizard, but one that I had never seen before or since.

"How you reckon that got put in there?" Lewis said.

"I don't know, but it's not a ruby; that's for sure," Charles said.

I looked at it, then turned to look at the destruction the lightning had done. The dead Osage warriors were in pieces. Limbs and bushes were burnt. Splinters were scattered and sticking in the ground. Yet, we were unharmed. How was it that we were not even blooded? We were not touched. Slowly I started to understand.

I took the red eagle from Charles and held it high. "*Wah-Kon-Tah!*"

They said nothing, just looked at me and the red bird.

I said it again as I shook it, "*Wah-Kon-Tah!*"

"It's not a god, you stupid Inyun," Lewis said.

"*Wah-Kon-Tah!*"

"Why *Wah-Kon-Tah*, John?" Charles said.

I turned toward the dead Osage warriors and swept my arm. "We were not scratched, but they are all dead." *Wah-Kon-Tah* is our greatest spirit. It is in everything. There is no doubt in my mind the spirit helped us.

Lewis felt of his body, as if he had not noticed he wasn't injured.

Charles turned back toward me. "There must indeed have been a spirit looking over us."

I don't know if Charles believed as I did, but he knew I believed it, and that was good enough for him.

I held the bird out to Charles. "*Wah-Kon-Tah.*"

He took the bird. "*Ca va.*"

Charles knew me better than any person alive. He understood me. He cared deeply for the Quapaw.

***

We buried the warriors in shallow graves and hung their possessions on poles above the graves. They would need them in the next life. By doing this, I hoped in the beyond they would be more friendly to the *O-Gah-Pah*. It was way into the night before we buried the last one. When we were finished, we made camp at the creek. We took dried meat from the warriors' bags and made our supper, but none of us ate much.

The storm had vanished as fast as it had appeared, and the stars shown bright as we sat around our little fire. We said nothing for a long time. We were tired and each of us was deep in our own thoughts. We had just seen men killed. I had almost scalped a man.

Lewis held the red eagle close to the fire. "Reckon what that little lizard is in there?" He licked the red bird and polished it with his arm before he held it close to the fire again. "Reckon how it got in there?"

"*Wah-Hun-Gah-Zhee*," I said as I shook my head.

"Yeah, that's right," Paul said. "He is crazy."

Paul held the shell pieces together, and examined them in the firelight. "This is not Cherokee or Quapaw."

I took them from him. The shell had been skillfully carved. I noticed the bird was the same bird as was on the red stone. They both looked as real as life—I had never seen such work.

"This all may have been fashioned by ancient Indians," Charles said. "We can imagine they camped right here on this very spot hundreds of years ago."

"Yeah, and they fought some other warriors, and before the last one died, they hid this in that tree," Paul said.

"Or, they were to return to get it, but were killed, and here it has remained," Charles said as he stood. "This spot could also be a sacred place on the prairie."

Paul jumped to his feet. "And that is why the lightning flashed and only struck the Osage warriors because we are chosen."

Lewis spit into the fire, and it hissed. "Chosen for what?" He examined the eagle again with the aid of the campfire.

Charles and Paul looked at each other, but had no reply.

"That's what I thought," Lewis said. "Now who is *Wah-Hun-Gah-Zhee*?" He raised his leg and farted. We scattered away from the fire until the air cleared. Lewis sat in it and laughed.

We gathered back around the fire, and I said, "It is *Wah-Kon-Ta*; I have no doubt."

Charles took the shell pieces from me. He handed one of the four pieces of the shell to each of us. "We all agree something special happened here, some special power, *oui*?"

We all agreed as we studied our shell piece.

"Look at us," Charles said. "We are all different. I don't see how we could be any more different: one Quapaw, one Negro, one Frenchman, one... Hell, Lewis, I don't know what you are."

We laughed. Lewis tried not to laugh, but couldn't help it. "I'm the only real American here."

"My point is we are all different, but we have been friends for a long time," Charles continued. "Today is a good example. We came together and defeated our enemy."

"I would say we had a little help," Lewis said.

"That's my point," Charles said. "We were chosen."

"Horse turds," Lewis said.

"Charles speaks true," I said. "If you had not dared him to climb that tall cypress, we would not have known the enemy was coming. Something made that happen."

"And why did we think we could defeat a band of Osage warriors?" Paul said. "Because we were chosen by...by... *Wah-Kon-Tah*." He reached down and took the eagle from Lewis and held it and his shell piece high in the air. "From this time forward, we should call ourselves the 'Red Eagle Band.'"

Lewis laughed. "That sounds ignorant."

Charles took the eagle. "How about 'The Order of the Red Eagle'?"

I took the bird from Charles and turned it over a few times in my hand. I thought about what they were saying, and I agreed. There was something special in our friendship. We had never wavered. We had always been loyal and true. That must have been noticed by the spirits looking down on us. The spirits had sent the lightning.

I raised the bird in the air. The firelight glimmered in it like magic. "I agree with Charles, but we will forever say it with *O-Gah-Pah* words: "The Order of *Khi-Dha'-Zhu'te*."

"What does that mean?" Lewis said.

Charles put a hand on Lewis's shoulder. "I think it means 'red eagle.'"

When morning came we put the bird back in the hollow tree, but we each kept our piece of shell. We agreed to not keep the shells on our body, but to hide them so we didn't lose them. About once a month, we would come back to the sacred spot and perform a little ceremony that we had agreed on and check to see if the struck tree was still alive. We would honor the Osage warriors, too. We did this even when we were grown men, and our friendship never wavered. I have never known friends before or since that were as true as we were.

***

"John, what happened to you and The Order of *Khi-Dha'-Zhu'te*?"

John stared into the fire, but said nothing.

"John?"

He slowly looked at me. "Let us sleep. We will go to the sacred place in the morning." He said nothing else as he made himself comfortable and closed his eyes.

I wallowed me out a soft spot and lay on my back looking at the stars. I was anxious and a little scared. I didn't know whether to believe the sacred stuff or not. But I had seen the shell pieces, and I knew something was very heavy on John's mind.

I looked at the stars and imagined them all those years ago when those boys ran wild on the prairie—this very prairie. I imagined my grandfather as a boy. Somewhere on that prairie many years ago ran my dreams as I fell asleep.

Chapter 8

John had us up and moving through the prairie as the eastern sky was just turning pink. He picked his way through the tall grass, said the old animal trails he remembered were no longer there, so we forged a new trail. We had gone about a half a mile when he stopped suddenly and smelled the air.

I walked up behind him. "What do you smell?"

"Hogs, horses, people."

We trekked on through the prairie; the tall grass gave way to shorter grass. We could see for miles, but I saw no hogs or horses. We came to a road, and John looked up it, then down it. He didn't like something about it.

"Is this the road where you attacked the Osage warriors?"

He turned to me. "It's the road. All those years ago, it was nothing more than a heavy trail." He pointed to the dirt. "Look at all the horse and wagon tracks. This road is well used."

We heard a dog barking up the road behind a clump of trees. John said nothing, just started in that direction. I followed.

We came to a small farm with cows and pigs about the place. A house set in the middle of a clearing with a small barn. Oak trees had been planted around the place; they couldn't have been planted more than ten years ago. There was even a peach orchard with a few late peaches. John walked over and picked one. I grabbed me one, too.

A man yelled from a cornfield. "Get off my peaches!"

I whirled and dropped my peach. John didn't turn. He picked another peach and bit into it.

"John, that man don't want us eating his peaches."

"The man only has a hoe," John said, but didn't turn to look.

"How do you know that? You haven't even looked at him."

John finished the second peach. "Saw him right off. He was hiding behind the corn."

The man was about seventy yards away, but marching toward us with his hoe raised and ready to swing.

"We didn't mean any harm," I said.

"I will show you, you thieving Indians," the man said as he picked up his pace.

In one motion John pulled an arrow from his quiver, nocked it to his bowstring, wheeled around, pulled, and released. The arrow stuck in the ground right in front of the man. He stumbled, then stopped.

"A peach is not value enough to die over." John nocked another arrow. "But if you think it is, so be it."

"No! No! I think not." The man dropped his hoe. "Take anything you like."

The man had made it to within forty yards of us when John stopped him with the arrow. He looked to be thirty or so, had on a coonskin cap, but half the tail was missing.

John lowered the bow to his side and walked to the man.

"Anything. Take anything," the man said.

John stopped in front of the man, pulled the arrow from the ground, and placed it into his quiver. "This your place?"

The man nodded.

"So, you don't mind if me and the boy eat a few more of your fruits?"

"No, not at all." The man eyed the bow.

"Get a few more peaches," John said to me without turning away from the man.

"Yes, get a handful," the man said.

I was shaking. I didn't know what was about to happen, but I picked five or six of the prettiest peaches from the nearest tree. I dropped them into my bag and turned back to the men.

"How many farms between here and the Arkansas Post?" John said. His hand was on his knife.

The man swallowed hard. "There are about ten between DeWitt and the Post."

"What is DeWitt?" John said.

The man hesitated, swallowed, then said, "It's the new County Seat." He pointed up the road. "It's about a mile up the road there; not much to it, courthouse, few houses."

John said nothing for a long time just stared at the man. Finally he said, "Any houses between here and DeWitt?"

"No, just useless prairie."

I went to John and gave him a peach.

John looked at the peach; then he looked back up to the man. He raised the peach. "*Merci*."

"Welcome." The man wiped the back of his trembling hand across his forehead.

John took a bite from the peach and started up the road; I followed. I looked back to see the man standing in the same spot, watching us leave. He stood there until I lost sight of him behind his young oaks.

"Reckon he will get a gun and come after us?" I said.

John retrieved another peach from me and slowly shook his head.

"How do you know this?"

John smiled, but didn't answered. He was right; the man never came.

We followed the rutted road. We appeared to be in a wilderness of grass, but for the road. After we walked a mile or so, we came to a stretch of woods. In it was a creek. Beyond we could hear more dogs barking. A narrow pall of smoke rose high in the air from that direction. John stopped in the road and stared at the smoke.

"What do you reckon it is?" I said.

He looked down at me. "Must be DeWitt, stuck in the middle of the prairie."

"Reckon we'll find out shortly."

"*Non.* We are here." John pointed to an odd-shaped tree. "That is the tree that was hit by the lightning."

I felt a sudden flutter in my chest. I believed his story, but in the back of my mind I guess I had doubted it a little.

John closed his eyes, whispered something I couldn't hear, then went to the tree and found the opening. Through the years it had almost grown over completely. He pulled his big knife and started carving away wood. My heart raced. He finally fashioned a hole big enough for him to get his hand into. He slowly pulled out a rotten cloth—it fell away as he pulled it from the tree. He turned toward me and held up the Red Eagle.

John sat flat on his butt. "*Khi-Dha' Zhu'te*," he whispered. He slowly wiped years of dirt and filth from the precious piece. Tears rolled down his weathered and creased face. He held it up to examine it. I moved closer and could see the little creature inside.

I could say nothing—I didn't know what to say. I didn't even know what to think. Was it really magic? What was that thing inside the stone? I couldn't control my breathing. It is about as close as I've ever come to fainting.

John whispered words to the red stone, but they were too soft for me to hear—it was some kind of prayer or chant. He raked the leaves and sticks back until he revealed dirt; then he drew a circle about a foot across. He placed the bird in the center, reached into his bag and brought out the pieces of the seashell. He stuck all the pieces together until the shell was whole and set it by the bird. All the while he kept up the prayer. He closed his eyes and raised his hands in the air, palms up.

I didn't know what else to do so I sat beside him as he chanted. There were a few words that I understood. He called out names: Paul, Lewis, Charles, John, and I believe many Indian names. There was one Quapaw word he said many times: *Akki-Kni*. After a while he got up and walked to a place a few feet from the tree and began his chant again. It dawned on me—this was the location of the Osage graves. He pointed in all four directions. Still speaking Quapaw, he repeated "*Akki-Kni*" several more times. Finally he sat down beside me again. "It has been a long time returning here, John Gillette." A weak smile appeared on his lips. "It has been a very long time."

"What do we do now?" I said.

He laughed and placed a hand on my shoulder. "We move away down the creek and away from the road and make a camp. I have many things to tell you."

***

It was a warm day, but it was cool next to the little creek and under the trees. We cleared us a little camp and ate on the peaches. John shot a big fish, so he built a small fire and we let it slowly roast and smoke. It was pleasant here, and I thought it must have been so when John and his partners roamed the prairies and creeks and before the white people began settling on the prairie. It was where they had camped that night so many years ago.

John rolled a log next to the fire, and we sat on it. We turned the fish when we reckoned it needed it. We were in no hurry.

John made a big sweeping motion with his arm. "My people, the *O-Gah-Pah*—the Quapaw as whites call us—called all of this land ours. Before the whites came, my people were a great nation. You could walk for many days and still be on our land."

I said nothing, just listened.

"By the time I was born, we were not as many. The white man's sickness had killed so many of my people. But we were still our own tribe, our own nation, in our own land." He turned the fish again. "When the French came, my people befriended them. They were always a good partner. They were true to the Quapaw. They are my other people." He stopped speaking and looked toward the creek. He wasn't looking at anything in this time—he was many years in the past.

I put another stick on the fire and waited for him to come back to now.

"When I was a small boy, my grandfather told me of buffalo hunts here on the prairie."

I remembered him telling me this before, but I let him tell me again.

"Now the buffalo are only in the far west. Nothing is the way it was in the old days."

I thought how I would like to see a buffalo on the prairie.

"When I was born in 1800, the Spanish possessed the Arkansas Post. They said they owned the land, but we knew we owned the land. There were always more Frenchmen and Quapaw around the Post than Spanish. My people got along with them all. Then the Americans came and that was a different story. They took. They signed treaties, then broke them."

I poked in the fire. I didn't know what to say.

"The Americans settled along the rivers first. Whatever they wanted, they took. We gave them more, then they took more than that. As I told you before, they drove my people south to live among the Caddo Indians. The Caddo didn't want us either. They were as cruel as any white man. The Quapaw suffered down there—starved. The people came crawling back to the Arkansas River, but it was no longer Indian land. There were a few whites that felt sorry for my pitiful people. They helped the Quapaw, but the government would not let the Indians stay. The white man sent my people west, and now my people are scattered among other nations out there. Now the white man has our land for all time."

I slowly looked at him. "It is a sad story. I could understand if you hated white people."

He didn't look at me. He turned the fish and looked into the small fire. "My father was a Frenchman, white. He was a good man. He was good to me and good to my mother. He was killed by a drunk Quapaw just before my people were sent south." He looked at me. "To hate whites would be to hate my father, to hate myself. Should I hate all Indians because one killed my father?"

I didn't know what to say, so I said nothing.

"Days before they were to force my people to live with the Caddo, we met at the tree of *Khi-Dha' Zhu'te*: me, Charles, Lewis, and Paul. We had made a pact to always rely on each other. The Red Eagle was our bond, the sinew that tied us together. I was twenty-six when we camped our last night here. We were no longer just boys. Me and Charles were married. Your father was just born."

I sat there and tried to imagine the four young men sitting around the fire figuring what to do with the terrible situation.

"Lewis wanted to fight anyone who tried to drive us off our land; it was always his answer. Paul didn't know what to do, but he was with us whatever we decided. Charles had been sending letters to the government, but it did no good. That night while we slept Charles slipped away. He had told Paul to keep us at camp two more days until he returned. When I awoke the next day and saw Charles gone, I figured he thought there was nothing else to be done so he departed, not wanting to face me. I was hurt and angry. I was out of my head and would not listen to Paul or Lewis. I left with venom in my heart. It was the last time I saw either of them until I reunited with Lewis a few days ago."

"You must have hated my grandfather."

"Your grandfather went to the White River to find his father for help. Together they built a plan to help my people. Charles's father, my uncle, was by then a wealthy man like my father. He knew important people, and he took it upon himself to go to Washington on our behalf."

"What happened?"

John stuck another stick into the fire.

"My great-grandfather couldn't find help in Washington?" I said.

John stood. "He had already been trying to recruit help for us. There were many who wanted the Quapaw pushed out because we lived on good farmland. Your great-grandfather was murdered before he even made it to the Mississippi River. That is how much they didn't want us in Arkansas." He sat beside me again and turned the fish. "I believe he was going to Washington to deed this land—his land—back to the Quapaw. We will never know."

"Why didn't my grandfather, Charles, look for you when

he came back and discovered you gone?"

He pulled the fish from the flame and propped the stick on a log. "He tried. They all three tried. I would not let them find me. I was full of poison toward anyone who wasn't Quapaw."

He picked the Eagle up and looked at it. "We made a vow the day of the storm, the day we found *Khi-Dha' Zhute*, that we would always protect the Quapaw, as we had that night when confronting the Osage. We were young and believed we could do anything if we banded together. We believed the Red Eagle and the storm had been a sign—we were chosen." He took a deep breath. "I broke the bond. The other three tried for years to find me, but I would not be found."

"Do you still think the Red Eagle was a sign? Do you still believe y'all were chosen?"

He stared off into nothing for a time, then said, "The Eagle has powers. We found that out later." He turned toward me. "I don't know where it came from or who made it. I don't know why it was made, but it has a purpose. We felt it. It has a pull on the soul that I cannot explain."

"Do you mean it is like a god?"

He shook his head. "No. But maybe sent by a god."

I felt a chill over my body when he said that.

"We were young, but we were not so simple to think we could defeat the world just because of *Khi-Dha' Zhute*. But when we were with it, we felt a hunger to do something good." He squeezed my shoulder. "You will know. You will feel it."

I felt a heavy weight on me, and I was suddenly afraid. He noticed, smiled. "The world must be better. We must do for those who can't do for themselves. People must live together in peace."

I swallowed. "Do you think if you had stayed with the other three, y'all could have made a difference? Would the

Quapaw still be here?"

"I don't know." He lowered his head. "But turning on my friends has haunted me since. It was years later when I learned Charles's father had died for my people. I was so very foolish."

I picked the fish up and pulled a piece from it. "White people shouldn't have taken your land."

He rubbed the back of his neck. "It has always been so. People always take from the weaker. Indians do this to other Indians. Whites do this to other whites. My people tried to be friends with the Americans, but they broke their promises, time and time again. They took our lands. We never fought the white man; we tried to be friends and share our land. They took it all without us firing one arrow."

He held the Eagle up again. "This is why we should always be true to each other. Always be true, John Gillette. When you have a true friend, and you know him to be just and true, honor him. And always do the right thing by your fellow man." He looked at me and softly smiled—it was almost feminine. I had never seen the look from him before. "We failed my people—I failed because I didn't believe in my friends or myself."

He raised the Eagle again. "There is a force in this beyond anything you can now understand. But it only comes forth when you believe in it. Use this to the best advantage, John."

He stopped speaking and I saw his nostrils working; he smelled something in the wind.

"What is the force? When will I—"

He raised his hand and interrupted. "Remember what I have said as you remember to breathe. You have a choice as you live, to do good or do bad, to make a difference or not." He looked straight into my eyes and said something very strange. "You are me, John Gillette. You are me."

Suddenly came the unmistakable clicks from revolvers.

John didn't seem to be surprised. He continued looking into my eyes, smiled and slowly nodded.

"Hold it right there, Indian, or I will put a big hole in you."

I turned to the see the scar-faced man that had attacked me below Clarendon. I turned to my right, and there was Yellow Hair.

"Well, if it ain't the boy who likes to scribble," said Scar. He pointed the revolver at John's head. "Pull that pig-sticker out real slow and toss it over here."

John did as he said, and Scar picked it up and tucked it into his belt.

Yellow Hair grabbed the bow and quiver and threw it.

"Y'all step away from that there fire," Scar said.

We hesitated.

"Now!" he said.

We stepped back.

"Hold up there," Scar said. "Indian, hand me that red thing in your hand."

John didn't move.

Yellow Hair pointed the revolver toward my head; John tossed Scar the Eagle.

"What do we have here?" Scar examined the piece. "I bet this will fetch good money down in New Orleans or somewhere abouts."

Yellow Hair smiled like an idiot.

Scar stuck the Red Eagle into a filthy bag he had hanging from his side. "The good man up the road there said y'all was a stealing his peaches. We don't take to redskins stealing peaches." He leveled the gun at John's head and pulled the trigger. Suddenly the air was filled with white smoke. My ears rung like bells and my head hurt. Below the smoke I saw John trying to get up from the ground.

I fell to my knees. "John!" I took hold of his arm. "John!"

He looked squarely into my eye—into my soul. He whispered, "*Akki-Kni*." Blood poured down the side of his head, but he smiled at me. "*Akki-Kni*."

I cried like a little boy. "What does it mean, John?"

Scar snatched me away.

John, still smiling, nodded.

Yellow Hair stepped closer to John and shot. Smoke bellowed again and John lay still.

I pulled free of Scar, but Yellow-Hair grabbed me and poked his gun barrel into my ear.

"Whoa!" Scar grabbed his arm and pulled the barrel away. "Didn't you hear what the Indian called him? 'John Gillette.'"

Yellow-Hair said nothing, just looked blankly at Scar.

"This boy's pa is that Gillette fellar that lives up on the White near DeValls Bluff. He might pay us to get the boy back." He smiled and nodded. "They's got a good spread, and they's got a little wealth about 'em."

Yellow Hair smiled and squeezed me.

"Come on," Scar said. "Let's go on down to the Post and meet up with Rufus. We can hang out there until the Yankees get off the White River. That old Cajun might be there that always buys purty stuff like this here red bird."

Yellow Hair pulled me as they went toward the road. I looked back at John. There was now a big pool of blood on his back. He would not have to worry about *Khi-Dha' Zhu'te* anymore. They will never drive him from Arkansas again.

"Can't we bury him?" I said, rubbing my eyes. I tried to pull free, but it was no use.

"The wolves will take care of him," Scar said, and they pushed me before them.

I looked back as they shoved me. I would never forget John. I would never forget the things he taught me.

***

As we walked by the farm with the peaches, I saw the man

lying dead, his coonskin cap still on his head. Yellow-Hair and Scar took no noticed as we walked on. They were good at killing, but they weren't much on burying. I figured they would have at least dragged him into the weeds. Curtains were hanging outside the windows, and broken furniture was scattered in the yard. They had been busy.

We walked south for about an hour or so through the prairie and came to a little hickory and oak grove. There was a small log cabin there, and we went in. The place smelled rotten. Someone had spilled grease on the wall by the fireplace. The place had smoke stains all in it where the chimney had once been stopped up. There was a chair made of sticks and slats, no table or bed, just the chair. Scar sat in the chair, and Yellow-Hair sat on the floor by the fireplace. I just stood there.

"Sit over there by that window," Scar said.

I sat down and fought hard to keep from crying. I was in a situation; I was miles from home. No one knew where I was, and now John was dead. I looked at my bag beside me. At least I still had my art. I felt relief for that, and just as quickly, I felt ashamed for thinking of it. Why was this happening? Why was I involved in this? I just wanted to go downriver to draw birds. I was just proving to my pa that I could manage without him. Now, I would give anything to be back home with him.

Scar pulled the Eagle from the bag. "What the hell is this thing anyhow?"

Yellow Hair shrugged his shoulders.

Scar examined it. He squinted and made contorted faces. A good sign of failing eyesight—I wished he was blind. He looked at the window, got up and walked to it. The late afternoon sun beamed through. He held the Red Eagle up to the window. The sun struck the red bird, and the thing glowed fire-red. It frightened me with the sudden change in color.

"What is that in there?" he said.

Suddenly Yellow Hair started yelling and scooting across the floor. I turned to see what the ruckus was all about. There was a large black lizard crawling on the floor.

Scar wheeled. "What's the matter with you?"

The lizard disappeared.

"There was a alligator or something on the floor!" Yellow-Hair said.

"You're touched in the head, boy. There ain't nothin' there."

Yellow-Hair got to his feet and looked all around. "It was there."

Scar became concerned and pulled his revolver. "What did it look like?"

"I told you—a alligator."

I had an idea what it was. "You know that red eagle has special powers."

Scar pointed his gun at me. "This here has powers, too."

I took a deep breath and mustered a little more nerve. "The Quapaw call that red eagle, '*Khi-Dha' Zhu'te.*'" I reached my hand out for it.

Scar pulled it to him.

"You have the gun. What can I do? I just want to look at it."

Scar looked down at the eagle, then slowly handed it to me.

I took the bird and studied it. The two men watched me. I started chanting gibberish. Slowly I did a little shuffle and chanted words that sounded as close to Quapaw as I could think up—I hoped they couldn't speak Quapaw. Those two idiots could barely speak English. I chanted and I looked to the roof and prayed in earnest to some native god. They looked at the roof to see what I was praying to. I held the bird up high and yelled "*Khi-Dha'-Zhu'te*!" a few times. Yellow Hair even muttered the words one time until Scar cut him a warning look. I danced around and chanted and prayed and chanted again. When I got close the window again, I yelled "*Khi-Dha' Zhu'te!*" at the top of my voice and heaved the Red Eagle into the sunbeam.

The bird glowed red again. The black lizard reappeared on the floor as the sunlight passed through the stone and cast a shadow of the little lizard within. The makeup of the stone made the sun dance in it, causing the black lizard to appear to be crawling across the floor.

As soon as I saw this, I yelled "*Khi-Dha' Zhu'te!*"

Both men saw the lizard.

Yellow Hair screamed and tried to climb the wall.

I yelled again, "*Khi-Dha' Zhu'te!*"

Scar shot the shadow twice with his revolver, filling the room with stinking smoke.

I pulled the stone from the sunlight. I acted faint and staggered a little. "I told you the stone has powers."

Scar snatched it from me, shot a hole in the window and threw it outside. His chest was heaving and he was as scared as a trapped rabbit.

Yellow Hair was crying. "We're screwed. We brought this on us by killing that Indian."

"Shut up!" Scar said, as he ran his fingers through his hair and walked around the room. He stopped suddenly and pointed the gun at me. "You brought that thing to life by saying them Indian words."

"Yeah," Yellow-Hair said. "You said them Indian words."

I had to think fast. I had seen how quick he was at pulling that trigger. "I'm the only one to stop it," I said. "Just because you threw it out the window ain't gonna stop it."

Scar looked at me for a long time without saying anything. He was studying on it. He pointed the revolver toward the door. "Let's go outside and you find that thing."

I dug around in the weeds for a while before I located it. I looked to see the sun was down below the trees. There would be no more magic today. But I now understood the force.

***

Scar decided we would stay the night in the cabin and continue on to the Post the next morning. They were to meet up with a man called Rufus. Scar started a fire in the fireplace, but it soon smoked up the cabin. He put the fire out and we opened the door to let the smoke escape.

Scar pushed Yellow Hair out the door. "Get a big stick to clean out the chimney."

A wasp popped Scar on the back. "Damn!" He swatted it with his hat and killed it.

Yellow Hair came in with a cane pole someone had left outside the cabin. He ran the pole up the chimney and pumped it a few times. A wasp nest the size of a pie plate flopped down on his head, and a wad of big orange wasps boiled off it. His head was soon covered with the angry wasps, and he swatted and screamed like a mad man. Scar and I fought each other to get out the door first. Scar got popped a few times. To this day, I don't know how I escaped without one sting. We ran down the road a good piece before we stopped.

Yellow Hair fell out the door screaming and flailing his arms. He saw us and ran toward us, leaving the swarm of wasps behind. When he got to us he was gasping. His eyes grew wide; then they rolled back and he collapsed. He lay on the ground quivering with a funny wheeze coming from his throat. It finally stopped and he moved no more.

Scar looked down at him for a time, but said nothing. He looked at the cabin. "Boy, you will have to go in there and get our stuff."

What kind of man was I dealing with? His partner had just

been killed, and he showed no more feelings than a toad-frog. I looked at him and shook my head.

He was handy with his revolver and stuck it in my face again. "Get our stuff."

"What do you intend to do?"

"You have poisoned this place with that Indian spell. I ain't staying here. It's already done gone and killed one man."

I looked down at Yellow Hair, then back up at him. I was not about to change his mind on the matter. If he believed Indian magic had caused this, the better for me.

The wasps had settled some, and I was able to get in and out quickly without getting stung. Scar believed it was because of my magic. Maybe. Maybe.

The shadows were long and the crickets singing when we headed south down the road. I was not keen on traveling down the unfamiliar road in the dark. I don't think Scar was either. He was worried about the Indian magic more than any animal that could attack us from the bushes.

The tall grass swayed in the wind as the darkness settled on the prairie. Scar kept walking and I kept walking with him. I hoped he would let his guard down. When he did, I would slip into the tall grass.

After a long walk, we smelled smoke. A little farther we saw a campfire.

Scar grabbed my arm. "You be a good boy. You say the wrong thing, the first thing I will do is shoot you. Understand?"

I gave him a "go to hell" look.

He put his hand on his revolver. "Understand?"

I wanted him dead. "I understand."

When we neared the camp, we saw three Confederate soldiers, one standing in the road watching us come.

"Stop right there!" the soldier said when we were within fifty yards of the camp. "Who are you and what is your business?"

"We ain't nothin' but a couple of travelers headed to the Post," Scar said.

The two other soldiers picked up their weapons and stood at the ready.

"Come closer," the soldier in the road said, "but keep your hands at your sides."

Scar whispered to me. "Remember, I will shoot you first."

The soldiers were satisfied that we were no threat, and the three of them asked us to join them in the camp. Somehow they had come across coffee, and offered us a little. To really say it was good coffee would be a stretch. No, it would be a damn lie. There may have been a little coffee in there, but it tasted a lot like rotten sweet potatoes. One of the soldiers grinned every time I turned up the tin cup.

Scar was a master at stretching the truth, said I was his son, and we were heading down to Natchez to see kin. Since I hadn't spoken, yet, he told them that I couldn't talk and gave me a glance while he ran his hand over his holster. I took his meaning.

A rumble could be heard in the west, and distant flashes told of an approaching storm. The soldiers talked about it and hoped it went around us.

Scar fell in with the soldiers as if they were old partners. They laughed and carried on while I kept my mouth shut.

They had beans cooking over the fire, and we joined in eating when the cook declared them soft enough to consume. I ate a few, but I wasn't hungry.

"These were some mighty fine beans." Scar said. "So good in fact, they done got me boilin' inside. Reckon I need to purge."

The soldiers laughed as Scar stepped into the tall grass.

I saw my chance. I slipped over to the nearest soldier. I whispered, "He's not my father. He has me held under threat of his gun. He's a thief and a murderer."

The soldiers readied their weapons for Scar to come out. They waited for a long spell, but he didn't show. One of them eased to the road and called out for him to come out and explain himself.

I will forever blame myself for what happened next. A bright orange light flashed, and a loud pop came from the grass. The soldier in the road hollered and fell to the ground. He twitched a couple of times, then moved no more. The other soldiers started shooting to where the flash had appeared. Suddenly another solder fell over dead. The last one took off down the road toward the Arkansas Post. Scar stepped out onto the road and shot at him a few more times, but I don't think he ever hit him as the soldier disappeared into the darkness.

"Damn it all!" Scar said.

He ran across the road and stuck the revolver in my chest.

I tried to say something, but could only stutter a few unrecognizable words.

He pulled the trigger. It clicked. He cocked the weapon again, and it clicked again. He hit me across the face with it. I saw white lights as I fell across one of the dead soldiers.

Scar mumbled and cussed as he fumbled with the loads and tried to reload the big revolver.

I stood and tried to regain my ability to speak, but nothing would come out. I couldn't think straight or I would have run into the grass. I could only think of that revolver being loaded to finish me off.

Scar fumbled with the gun and finally got a cap placed on the nipple. He cocked it and stuck it between my eyes. It felt like a hammer when the gun barrel hit my skull.

His chest was heaving as he screamed at me, "No one comes it over on me!"

I stammered, but I could not get out what I wanted to say.

I don't even remember what I wanted to say, but I figured I was about to die.

Scar lowered the gun. "No. I'm not gonna kill you now. I will just have to change my plans." He slapped me. "We can't go to the Post. That soldier will get there before us. Damnation!"

He rummaged around the soldiers' bags and found a short piece of rope. He tied my hands behind my back, then tied me to one of the dead soldiers.

"I'm gonna get a little sleep; then we are striking out back up the prairie," Scar said. "If you have any brains, you will sleep, too."

He kicked the fire out and moved across the camp into the darkness.

I stretched the rope to get away from the dead man I was tethered to. I couldn't get comfortable, nor did I care if I did as I lay on my side.

I had started out on an adventure because I was angry with my father. It seemed ridiculous as I lay there. In just a few days, my whole world had changed. I lived in a small cup of life. It was a sober awakening when that cup was poured into the larger bowl.

That night I watched the lightning flash back toward the west, followed by the rumble of thunder across the prairie, and I wept.

Chapter 9

It was still dark, but the morning birds had already started singing and peeping when Scar kicked me in my side. He cut the ropes from me and jerked me to get to my feet. I rubbed the rope burns as I noticed the lightning still carrying on in the west—strange that it hadn't moved.

"Boy, you pull the first shine, I'll kill you," Scar said. "Now move, and don't slow me down. We need to get some distance from here."

"Where are we going?"

He pushed me before him. "We're gonna cut across to Rock Roe on the White and find us a boat to get us to your pappy's farm."

We had a long walk ahead of us. I didn't believe I would ever see home again.

"Yessir, I'm gonna get a good return for you. I know you Gillettes are well to do."

I said nothing, just kept a good pace in front of him.

"How did you come to be out on the prairie with that Indian anyhow?"

I said nothing. He gave me a shove in the back.

I wanted to kill the man. I felt helpless, but I wanted to kill him.

"Answer me, boy."

"He captured me on the White River."

"Captured you? For what purpose?"

I could think of nothing.

He shoved me again.

"He needed me for a ritual of some kind."

"A ritual? What fashion of ritual?"

I thought for a minute, then decided I would feed him what he wanted. "He had that sacred bird, *Khi-Dha' Zhu'te*. He needed a boy my age to complete his ritual." I turned. "You saw its powers."

He was silent for a time. No doubt he was remembering the incident at the cabin.

"We were going to perform the ritual last night, but you came."

"Yeah, that's right. Now without the ritual, the bird has no power."

I laughed. "That's not how it works."

"What do you mean by that? Don't stutter with me, boy"

Lightning flashed in the west, but closer. The thunder followed with a rumble that shook the ground.

"Today is the very day that the gods of the Indians returned to the prairie." I was ashamed how easy the lie came to me, but it was necessary. "The Indian said the gods had been gone for over a hundred years, but today they returned. That is why he was back."

Scar laughed, but it was weak. "Back for what?"

"Back to channel the spirits of the gods. He said they would destroy every living person if they were not appeased. The spirit in *Khi-Dha' Zhu'te* has always been a reminder. That's what you saw in the cabin. The creature within is a warning."

I looked back and he was making sure his bag that held the eagle was closed.

"The gods will be looking for their people, but they will find no Indians on the prairie. They will be extremely angry."

"I had nothing to do with driving the Indians from Arkansas." He looked around the sky.

"You killed the one that had returned, the one that was here to appease the gods and tame the spirits."

"Shut that foolishness up!"

"You asked me—"

"I said be quiet about it."

I turned away and smiled. I believed he was buying it lock, stock, and barrel.

***

At daylight we arrived back at the cabin. Yellow-Hair's body was not in the road, but we found what was left of it in the edge of the grass. The wolves can do a horrible job on a body. Even Scar had to look away.

"Can't we rest at the cabin for a spell?" I said.

"No. Keep moving."

I noticed Scar kept looking behind us. And once when a prairie chicken flushed from the edge of the road, he almost screamed.

The wind picked up and the storm grew closer. The tall grass whipped and fanned. "We should stay in the cabin until the storm passes," I said.

"Keep moving and shut up."

He was afraid of that cabin, and not because of the wasps.

I had him convinced of the spirits.

We went on down the road as the wind grew. Suddenly a wolf howled beside the road. We both wheeled toward that direction.

"Just a wolf. Just a wolf." Scar was trying to reassure himself, but he was becoming terrified. He pulled his revolver and kept it in his hand as we walked.

When we made it back to the little farm, the murdered man was still on the ground where we last saw him. The wolves had not found him, yet.

"Let's go into the house," I said. "You can rest and there may be food."

Scar placed the gun back into the holster as we stepped upon the porch and scanned around the farm. "Go on in."

They had broken a good many things in the house, but the kitchen appeared to be waiting for the owner to return, which he never would. There was bread and a water pitcher on the table. The bread was a little hard, but that made little difference to us as we wolfed it down. We found potatoes and carrots in a pantry—we ate them raw.

Scar found a pipe on a shelf with fresh tobacco in it. The little house soon filled with smoke.

We sat across the table from each other. Scar was starting to relax—guess it was the tobacco. I studied him and tried to figure what to do next.

A weak voice came from the back room. "*Akki-Kni.*"

Scar jumped from the chair, dropping the pipe to the table.

My heart raced.

"*Akki-Kni.*"

Scar pulled his revolver. "It's the spirit!"

I looked at him, then looked at the closed door to the back room. I was beginning to believe it myself.

Scar pointed the revolver toward me. "Go check it out."

A moan came from the room.

I was afraid to go, so I stayed in the chair.

"Go!" He cocked the gun.

I went to the door. I swallowed, said a little prayer and opened the door. It was John. He was still alive lying across the bed. I ran to him. "John! It's me, John Gillette."

He opened his eyes, smiled weakly.

Scar came to the door. "Move back." He aimed the revolver toward John.

I turned and blocked his aim. I had to think fast. "Don't shoot. He is the only thing keeping the spirit of *Khi-Dha' Zhu'te* off us!"

Suddenly lightning flashed outside, and thunder cracked like a whip.

Scar almost dropped the gun. He looked at the window; then back to me, but said nothing.

I was breathing deeply—I couldn't seem to get enough air, but I didn't take my eyes from Scar.

He said, "Tend him, but if he gets outta that bed, I will finish him." He stepped back out of the room, but watched me through the doorway.

I opened John's shirt. There was blood everywhere, but it was not fresh. I put my ear to the wound, but neither heard nor felt air. The bullet went high and missed the lung. There was a wound on his head, but it was minor.

I turned to Scar. "Bring me some water."

He hesitated but left the doorway.

I pulled John's shirt from him. "I will get you patched up. I believe you will be fine."

John nodded, then took hold of my arm. "Do you have *Khi-Dha' Zhu'te*?"

"It's safe."

John let go my arm, relaxed, and whispered, "*Merci beaucoup*, John Gillette."

I stroked his hair. "You're welcome, John Gillette." I wiped the tears from my face.

Scar sat the water pitcher from the table on the floor by the door and backed out of the room as if John's wound were contagious.

I did the best I could for John—I was no doctor, nor knew much about such things. He was hot so I reckoned he had a fever. I tried to cool him down with a wet rag. His breathing was strong, and I believed he would survive; but I still had Scar to deal with. He could come in with that big revolver any minute. He was not beyond using it at a twinkling.

John started talking out of his head. "*Akki-Kni.*" He said it a few more times before he fell into a sound sleep.

I left him resting on the bed and went to face Scar.

"Well?" Scar said. He was perched at the table again, puffing on the pipe. "He gonna live or not?"

"I believe he will. You better hope he does. We don't want that spirit on us," I said as I sat across the table from him.

He pointed the pipe toward me. "I been thinkin' on that. I don't believe there is no spirit." He placed the pipe back into his mouth and talked over it. "This ain't nothin' but a storm."

"What about that monster back at that cabin? And those wasps? What about that?"

"Them hornets was just hornets, and that monster was just a trick you conjured up."

"A trick?" I spread my arms. "I did no trick."

I changed the subject before he got the idea of going in there and shooting John. "There are beans in the barrel by the fireplace. How about I get some cooking?"

Scar looked at the barrel, then at the window and the wind whipping outside.

"It will be raining soon," I said. "We may as well wait the storm here in this dry house."

He nodded. "I'm gonna be fartin' like a mule."

I grabbed a bucket and started out the door.

He raised the revolver.

"I have to get water to boil the beans."

He motioned toward the door with the revolver. "Go. I will be watching."

I went outside and he walked to the door. The wind was howling across the prairie, and black clouds rolled in the sky; everything looked yellow. Lightning cracked throughout the north and west. I'd never seen a storm move so slow, if it were moving at all. I pulled a bucket full of water from the well while looking at the tall grass beyond the house. In places it was taller than a man. I could easily escape through it. Scar was looking across the prairie and had taken his eyes from me. I could not leave John in there wounded. I went to the house with the water.

***

By the time the beans were cooked, it had grown late. John was doing better, but he was still sleeping a lot. I believed the fever was leaving.

Scar dug into the beans. An old sow made less noise.

I took a bowl in to John. He was awake when I went in. "Reckon you can eat a few beans?"

"*Oui.*" He tried to sit up, but grimaced.

I sat the bowl down on a small table by the bed and helped him up. It was a struggle for him, but he was able to take the bowl.

He looked toward the door. "How many?"

I held up one finger.

"The other?"

"Dead," I whispered.

He didn't ask what happened to the other man. He started eating.

Scar appeared at the door, looked in, then went back into

the other room. He had found the pouch of tobacco and kept the house smoked up.

Scar called from the other room, "Boy, come here."

John looked into my eyes. "Easy." He smiled.

I smiled back as I left the room. It was the only good feeling I had known lately.

Scar was looking out the window toward the road. "Go out there and drag that man into the weeds."

"You do it."

Scar wheeled and pulled the gun in one motion. I was a fool. John had just told me to be easy. He cocked the hammer.

I went out the door. It had begun to sprinkle, big heavy drops. I grabbed the man's arms. He had become stiff. I dragged him into the weeds as I was instructed. He looked like some kind of wooden man, one of his arms cocked and pointing into the air.

It is strange how a person can become calloused. When I pulled that man out of the road, I thought no more of it than if he were a dead possum. But I remember thinking how I bet a few days ago this man would have never dreamed this would have happened to him. I should have buried the man, but I knew Scar would not let me look for a shovel.

I had no sooner crossed the road back toward the house when a horseman rode up on a sweaty, black horse. He reined his horse up next to me. It was a Confederate captain. "How do?" he said. He took his hat off and mopped his forehead "You see any soldiers pass this way?"

I knew that deadly revolver was pointed straight at the captain.

"No, sir. No one has passed this way today."

He crammed his hat back on, rose up in the saddle and looked down the road, then back toward the house.

I prayed under my breath that this man didn't want to go

in the house.

He turned and saw the flashing lightning behind him. He looked down at me. "You have any warm food in the house?"

Before I could answer, lightning flashed and thunder cracked. He had to fight to control his wild-eyed horse.

"Never mind," he said. "I better ride if I want to get to the Arkansas Post before the bottom falls out." He looked toward the clouds. "I've never in my born days seen such a strange storm." He turned back to me. "Maybe the men had turned back because of the storm." With that he put spurs to the horse and was soon lost to the distance.

I washed my hands at the horse trough, then went back inside as the big rain drops increased.

"You just saved that man's life," Scar said. He smiled revealing yellow and black teeth.

I stopped and looked at him with disgust, pushed past and fixed me a bowl of beans.

***

While sitting in a chair by John's bed, I had fallen asleep. I awoke not knowing where I was. I rubbed my eyes; the room was strange and dark with only the dim light of a lamp from another room.

"You slept for a while," John said.

Everything—every event that had happened since I had left home came to me like a cold slap. I reached for John's hand. "How are you?"

"I will be fine, but the bad man is pacing the floor like a caged animal. He looks in often."

I looked toward the door. "How long did I sleep?"

John squeezed my hand. His strength was good. "A long while."

The rain was pouring now, and the storm was raging outside.

I turned toward John. "What do we do?"

His face was sculpted by dark shadows from the distant lamp glow. "We do as the panther: we make every muscle ready to serve, then we wait for a weak moment, a mistake, by our prey."

It's strange how everything can change with a simple statement. I had thought we were at Scar's mercy, but John saw it differently—Scar was at ours—he just didn't know it. For the rest of my life, I tried to always take that point of view, always be the aggressor.

Suddenly we heard a horse outside, then someone pounded on the outside door.

Scar appeared at the bedroom door. "Boy, go to the door and turn them away. I don't care who they are; you turn them away."

"How can you turn someone away on a night such as this?"

"You just do it!" He pulled at his hair as he thought, then looked at me. "Tell them the fever is in the house and many are sick."

John squeezed my hand, then released it. The gesture spoke volumes.

The man at the door looked like a drowned polecat. "I need to come in and dry off," he said.

"I'm sorry, but I can't let you in. We have the fever—"

He shoved past me into the room. He found a gun waiting for him. Slowly a smile grew on his face. "You wouldn't shoot your partner, would you?"

Scar lowered the gun and smiled. "I 'bout shot you, Rufus."

I closed the door and took up a position at the bedroom door.

Rufus started shucking clothes as he dripped onto the floor. "What you got here?"

"Waitin' out the storm."

"Where's Franklin?"

"He was stung to death by hornets."

Rufus stopped as he was pulling down his pants. "Don't you jaw me like that."

"I'm square. He's dead."

Rufus kicked the pants across the floor and sank into a chair with his dripping drawers. "He was my last brother."

"I buried him proper," Scar said. He glanced at me with a warning.

I held my tongue, but I could see the new boss had arrived.

"I got bushwhacked by some soldiers is why I didn't make it to the Post," Scar said as he sat down at the table.

"Yeah. You let one get away, and now they will be coming for you in the morning."

"Damnation!" Scar said.

"I struck out when the soldier came in a cryin' about it." Rufus stood and pulled his drawers off and laid them across a chair.

"Where did you get the horse?" Scar said.

Rufus pulled a rag from a hanger and dried his naked body. "From a dead captain between here and the Post."

"A dead captain?"

Rufus smiled. "He is now."

Scar laughed as he gathered the wet clothes and hung them around the fire.

Rufus looked at me. "This the owner of this here house?"

Scar pointed at me. "This here is our payday."

Rufus studied me up and down. "How so?"

"This here is Mr. Gillette."

Rufus scratched his butt. "Why, this ain't one of them Gillettes that owns all this land around here is it?"

"His pa has a place up around DeValls Bluff."

"Aw yeah; I knew his grandpappy, Monsieur Charles Gillette—the French bastard. He accused me of stealing his trees."

"Why would he do that?" Scar said.

"He caught me on his land cutting them up for riverboat firewood."

They both laughed at the ignorant joke.

"So, we gonna trade him for money?" Rufus said.

"That's my figurin'." Scar said.

"What sorta money you figurin' on?"

"I ain't studied on no particular amount, yet."

Rufus walked up to me with his naked body. He rubbed his beard. "I bet them Gillettes is got some gold or silver goodies, better'n any old Confederate butt paper."

"Rufus, you're botherin' me a walkin' around with your ass showin' like that." Scar grabbed his bag. "I got some more drawers in here." He pulled them out and the Red Eagle fell to the table.

Rufus took the drawers and pulled them on while looking at the eagle. "What's that?"

Scar pointed at it. "The boy had it. I was gonna try to sell it, but that thing has evil spirits in it."

Rufus picked it up. "You done lost your mind? There ain't no spirits one way or tother."

Lighting flashed and thunder cracked. The house shuttered and the dishes rattled.

Scar put his hand on his revolver as if it would help. "I told you!"

"Pshaw. It's just a storm like any tother."

Rufus took the eagle to the lamp to inspect it. "What's that inside there?"

"That's the spirit," Scar said.

"Tain't no damn spirit, I done told you." Rufus held it

closer to the lamp. "Looks like a lizard or tiny alligator." He raised it up and smiled. "Tain't nothin' but some old Indian whatnot. Might fetch a few coins if we're lucky."

Scar rubbed his head. "I don't know. It sho is mighty queer."

Rufus went to the window and looked out. He set the Red Eagle on the window sill. "Soon as this storm lets up, we gotta travel. They'll be comin' from the Post lookin' for you."

"I hope it lets up soon," Scar said.

Rufus turned from the window. "What the hell?" He reached for his gun on the table. John had appeared at the bedroom door.

"It's fine—It's fine!" Scar said. "I forgot about him, but he's done been shot good. He can't do nobody no harm."

"Who is the Indian?" Rufus said as he put his revolver back on the table.

"He's with the boy."

"Step out into the light, so I can see you better," Rufus said.

John didn't move.

Scar pulled his revolver again. "You heard him, Indian."

John stepped into the room.

"A stinkin' Quapaw," Rufus said. "I thought it was a real Indian."

John showed no emotion.

"How did you get by us? I thought we ran all y'all out of Arkansas."

I took John's arm.

"You're right," Rufus said. "I'd be worried if it was an Osage or even a Cherokee, but nobody gives a damn about a pitiful Quapaw."

John's face was iron, but I was steaming and did not hide it.

"Take him back in there," Rufus said. "I don't want to be bothered by him. They stink worse than a dog."

Scar waved his gun and we went back into the bedroom. I slammed the door, but Scar opened it back up.

We sat on the bed. "I'm sorry he talked about your people like that," I said.

He smiled. "Like the panther."

I smiled back and nodded. I had to be more like him. He was strong—strong inside.

***

The storm was relentless. The wind howled and drove the rain into the glass so hard, I believed it would break any moment.

John began singing a song under his breath—just a whisper. I could not hear the words. He swayed as he sang. He closed his eyes and seemed to be lost in another time. I watched him, but said nothing. I tried to imagine his world, tried to think what I would do if I had been tossed out of my home and away from everything I knew. I could not dream a dream as bad as his people's situation. How long had they been in Arkansas? No one knew for sure. But we knew when they were driven out. We know the exact date. I was not there, but I could imagine the suffering and the—

Lightning shot through the windows in a long bright burst. The thunder cracked like an explosion. As soon as the sound had left, the lightning started again.

Someone yelled in the other room. I jumped from the chair and ran to the door.

Rufus was backed up against the wall, screaming like he was being tortured. Scar was pulling at his revolver, but it would not clear his holster—he was white.

The Red Eagle in the window was glowing and sparkling. The creature crawled across the floor and up the wall. Every burst of lightning would make it move and appear in a different place. The sound of a wild animal wailed outside—panther or some other wild creature.

The thunder rattled the house like an earthquake. The lightning made the creature come alive. The men behaved as children. Then as quickly as it began, it was over. The house grew dark again, except for the subtle light from the lamp.

"I told you!" Scar screamed. "I told you it had spirits in it.!"

Rufus said nothing. He stood there in nothing but drawers and shook like a cold dog.

Scar grabbed the eagle, opened the door, and threw it. But he didn't move after he threw it. He was frozen in place.

I looked past him. The lightning flashed. An Indian stood in the dooryard. I saw a bow. I saw buckskin.

Scar slammed the door and shoved past me into the bedroom. "Who's out there?"

John said nothing.

Scar went back into the other room. "Get your clothes on, Rufus. We will have to get out of here. There is another Indian or spirit out there. I don't know what's going on, but I ain't waitin' on it."

Rufus had composed himself from the scare. "You're right. We need to get the hell out of here." He began pulling on clothes. "Did the Indian outside have a gun?"

"Just a bow and arrow," Scar said as closed his bag.

"If I see him again, I will put a bullet in his head," Rufus said. "I will take my chances with the storm and that stinking Indian, but I don't want nothing to do with that damn Indian spirit."

"I told you!"

"Shut up! Go out there and saddle the horse."

"Why did you take the saddle off the horse?"

"Just go get the damn horse saddled up."

"Who's gonna ride?"

Rufus grabbed Scar by the shirt. "We will both ride." He shoved him toward the door. "Now go saddle the horse."

Scar pulled his hat down to his ears and went out the door.

Rufus yelled out to the darkness, "If you bother my man, I will kill the Indian and the boy." Then he strapped his revolver on and looked at me. "Get whatever bags you are carrying, and let's go. The wounded Indian stays or I will kill you both."

"It's storming outside. You two are fools," I said.

He stormed around the table and grabbed my arm. "I don't want no lip from you, boy. You knew that thing was a spirit, and you let it out on us."

Suddenly we heard that wild creature outside scream out again. Rufus let go of my arm. "What the hell is that?"

It sounded like a panther, but I saw my chance to make more of it. "It's the creature you released from the stone."

Rufus looked at me, but said nothing; then he looked at the window.

Two shots rang out.

Rufus pulled his revolver. He looked at the door, then turned and grabbed me. "You stay right with me. Don't do anything stupid or I will kill you."

"Rufus!" Scar yelled from outside. "Rufus! There is something out here. It ain't no Indian." He was hysterical.

"Come back in!" Rufus yelled. "We will wait 'til daylight to strike out."

Three more shots blasted outside. Then no other sound but distant thunder. The wind had died and the rain had suddenly stopped.

"Come on back in!" Rufus yelled.

There was no reply.

Rufus pulled me close. "What is that thing?" He shook

me. "What is that thing?"

I was becoming scared now. I didn't have an answer.

The door slowly opened. Scar was standing there in the dark, barely lit by the lamp.

Rufus released me. "Don't stand there, fool. Come in and shut the door."

The animal shrieked again from outside.

Scar fell into the room.

I jumped. I felt myself shaking.

Rufus grabbed Scar's arm and pulled him into the room. Then he slammed the door. He bent down and rolled Scar over. Scar's face was frozen in a state of terror, but he was dead. Rufus stood and stared at Scar's face. Rufus trembled with fright.

The door flew open.

Rufus pulled his gun and shot twice at the darkness.

He reached over and pulled me to him, putting the gun to my head. "I've got this boy. I will kill him if you don't let me alone."

The distant lightning lit up the dooryard, and we saw something large stand there before it grew dark again. Rufus shot three more times out the door, but the lightning and figure were gone when the lightning flashed again.

Rufus began breathing hard.

I was confused and scared.

"Who are you?" he screamed. "Who are you?"

From behind us came softly, "*Wah-Kon-Tah.*"

We both turned.

John was standing there with his arms spread. "*Wah-Kon-Tah.*"

Rufus raised his gun to shoot. "Shut up, you filthy Indian."

Suddenly he lurched. There was an arrow through his body, the bloody stone point protruding out the other side.

He looked at the arrow sticking from his chest, then looked at John.

John looked into his eyes as deeply as I've ever seen a man look into another man's eyes. "*Wah-Kon-Tah.*"

Rufus's blood spewed from his chest, and he just stood there turning white. Air wheezed from the holes.

The front door shut.

I turned. It was a big Indian with red paint striped down his face. He was holding a bow in his hand. The bow looked familiar. There was the knot—it was John's bow. I looked closer at the Indian. It was no Indian—it was Lewis. But it was not the big sloppy Lewis that we had left at Maddox Bay. This Lewis was erect—he was regal.

Slowly, Rufus staggered and the gun fell from his hand. It hit the floor. There was an explosion, pain, then darkness.

Chapter 10

When I awoke, my head felt like it was between a hammer and an anvil. I reached up and felt a bandage wrapped around it. Sunlight fought through a dirty window, and someone was whacking, maybe chopping wood. I was confused, didn't know where I was, and the last thing I remember was Scar smoking a pipe at that house. The room that I was now in looked familiar, but I was still confused. Something brushed my hand, then licked it. I turned. It was General Jackson.

"Why, you're awake." Mr. Stilman was sitting at the table drinking his Sassafras brew—the smell drifted to me with his words.

I blinked my eyes a few times. I was trying to get some understanding of what was happening.

"I knew you would be about any day," Mr. Stilman said. "Yep, I called it."

The chopping stopped outside. The porch boards creaked; then Lewis stepped in the door. "Mr. Stilman, you called it,"

Lewis said. "You said he would come back to the world of the living today, and here he is."

Mr. Stilman slurped his brew and nodded. "Yep."

I remembered rain—lightning—a storm. Suddenly a pain shot around my head like fire. I grabbed at the bandage.

"Whoa, Partner," Lewis said as he took hold of my hand. "Easy. You got a gunshot wound to the head. Take it real easy."

Mr. Stilman got up from the table and fluffed my lumpy pillow.

I looked at Lewis with his big nasty beard and his rough, old face. I now remembered him at the house with the storm. But this was not that Lewis. That Lewis had red paint on his face. He was stronger, taller, younger. He wore buckskins, not these old nasty clothes.

I felt dizzy. I looked around the room, but it began to spin. I saw faces. I saw our farm back at DeValls Bluff. I remembered pulling the pirogue from the barn. The room spun faster. I remembered the first time I saw John. John! Where was John? The room turned faster and faster and faster...

"*Akki-Kni.*" I heard the words, but saw no one saying them.

"John? Where are you?" I said.

I heard Lewis tell Mr. Stilman to get a wet rag, but the voice was far away—it was in a well.

"*Akki-Kni.*" The voice came from every corner of the room.

"Where are you, John?"

"*Akki-Kni.*" The voice came from the window.

"John?"

"*Akki-Kni.*" The word softly echoed around the room, then faded away.

"John, where are you? What does it mean?" I wanted to sit

but I could not move. "John?" Everything went dark.

***

I awoke again and felt something tickling my nose. I opened my eyes to see two small, round eyes looking at me. It was the mouse. I now knew where I was. I smiled. "Making your rounds?" The mouse jumped from the bed and disappeared into some secret hiding place.

I took a deep breath and ventured to sit up. I was a little shaky, but, all and all, not too bad. The wood floor was cool on my bare feet; it was refreshing. I stood. There was a rush to my head, but it soon passed. I felt the bandage. I walked to the open window and took a deep breath. I felt my strength gaining. I saw no one outside, not even the dog.

I went out to the porch in my drawers. The rocking chair was inviting, so I sat in it and looked out across the yard—the woodpile, poison ivy growing up a few of the trees—and thought Mr. Stilman must have spent many a day rocking here alone and looking at the same view.

I reckoned Mr. Stilman would spend the rest of his life at this cabin hiding from life. But maybe this was the life he wanted. You never know what another man thinks or desires. That's one of the faults of man: to judge, to try to make our desires someone else's desire.

A mockingbird swooped in front of me and landed in a little possum haw tree. It had some sort of big, green worm in its beak. I spotted the nest. The bird worked its way to the nest, and four mouths shot up from it, each begging for the juicy worm.

I went in and looked for my bag. I prayed under my breath that nothing had happened to it. I found it in a corner with my clothes on top of it; they had been washed.

I put my clothes on and returned to the rocking chair with my tablet and pencil. It was good to draw again. It was my tonic. It was my magic. The pencil felt good in my fingers, like a cool drink to the soul.

The mockingbird is a brave bird. It was not bothered by me at all. Soon the mate came and they busied themselves fattening up the chicks. They came in with bugs that I had never seen before—strange-colored ones, too.

Soon the flow was back. I sketched at a mad pace—you have to be fast when your subject is fast. I felt my strength return with every scribble. I felt my soul bloom back into fullness with every line and dot. This is who I am; this is what I am.

Time lies to you when you are caught up in something you love. When the birds stopped coming, I noticed the sun had moved a good bit. As I put my things away, I wondered where the others were.

I thought about yelling, then spotted General Jackson galloping across the yard. He ran to me and licked and rubbed against me until he was patted thoroughly. Soon Lewis and Mr. Stilman appeared in the clearing, Lewis carrying a stringer of fish.

Mr. Stilman turned to Lewis. "I told you the boy would be up and about soon. I knew it when the fever broke."

Lewis smiled and nodded. "You called it."

"How you feeling?" Mr. Stilman said as he stepped up on the porch.

"Well. I feel well."

"How's that head?" Lewis said from the yard.

I touched the bandage. "Doesn't hurt much at all."

Lewis grinned big. "Good." He raised the fish. "Hungry?"

I realized I was starving. The last thing I had eaten was a bowl of beans. Suddenly I realized that I didn't know how long ago that had been or how long I had been at Mr. Stilman's place.

Lewis must have recognized the puzzled look on my face. "You should be starving. You've been out for four days. We gave you water, but that's all."

"Four days?"

"That's right," Mr. Stilman said. "You came around two days ago, but you went right back out."

I remembered. Suddenly, I thought of John. "Where is John?"

Mr. Stilman looked at Lewis.

Lewis tied the fish to a nail stuck in the porch post. "He didn't come back with us."

I looked toward the prairie. I didn't understand.

"I'm gonna start a fire," Mr. Stilman said. "I got some bear grease, and we gonna have some good fish cooked up pretty soon." He took the fish from the nail and glanced at me before going in the house.

"Is he all right?" I said.

"He'll be fine," Lewis said.

"Where is he? Why didn't he come back here? I thought John liked me," I said.

Lewis smiled. "Oh, I reckon he likes you fair enough."

"Where is he, Lewis? What's he doing?"

He sat on the edge of the porch and scratched his head. "I reckon he's still searching for what he lost thirty years ago." He thumped an ant from the porch. "I can't rightly say what he's doing. You could sooner catch a weasel than figure out that Inyun."

I stepped off the porch and started across the yard.

"Where you going?" Lewis said.

I said nothing, just kept walking. I don't know why, but I felt betrayed by John. He should have been there when I woke up.

John fell in behind me. "Boy, you's too weak to be traipsing around like that."

I kept walking and thinking. I reckon I really didn't know John after all. How could I? I only met him a few days ago.

Lewis was talking to me as we walked, but I didn't really hear him.

He grabbed my shoulder. "Where you going, boy? You gonna just walk across the prairie like a fool?"

The prairie was there before us, green and brown. I had never thought much of it before, just a bunch of grass. John had changed that, made me appreciate it and the Indians that once called it home.

"Lewis, could y'all have done anything for the Quapaw?" I turned to him. "Could y'all have made a difference?"

Lewis smiled, but it was a sad smile. "Naw." He squeezed my shoulder. "It was too big. We all knew it, except John, but we would not give up trying. We would do anything for John and the Quapaw. We could not stop the cyclone that was pushing the Indians out of Arkansas, too many big bugs, the government."

"And John blames himself for it all," I said as I sat on the ground.

"I don't know." Lewis grunted and sat beside me. "I reckon John knew it deep inside, but he needed hope, so he believed more and more that the Red Eagle was magic."

"You don't think it has powers? How do you explain the creature?"

Lewis pulled a piece of grass and poked it into his mouth. He took a deep breath and slowly let it out. He paused for a few minutes; then looking across the prairie, said, "It has powers; that's for sure." He took the grass from his mouth and turned to me. "But it ain't magic."

"What is it then?"

"Your grandfather, Charles, was a good deal smarter than me, but he never figured it out either. Paul was the one that nailed the hide to the barn. He said it was like sinew."

"Sinew?"

Lewis smiled. "Yeah. Indians use it to tie the points and

feathers on the arrow. They make a strong string out of it."

I nodded. "I know what it is. It's made from animal tendons. It's also used to make bow strings."

"That's the long and short of it," Lewis said. "By its lonesome, it ain't much; but when you use it to make stuff, it has worth."

"I don't follow you. What do you make with the Red Eagle?"

Lewis pulled another grass stalk. "You don't make nothing with it, but for some reason, it draws you in. It binds you to it. Everybody is pulled to it like a moth to a fire."

"Maybe that's the magic."

Lewis spit out the grass. "John thought so. He wanted to help his people, and he got it in his head that red stone was the symbol of his effort. It was the sinew that held our little band together, the sinew that held our cause together."

I thought on it for a time, but I still believed there was more to it than that. "What about the creature?"

Lewis didn't answer.

"What about that night during the storm? You were different. You seemed younger, stronger."

Lewis stood as the wind picked up and the prairie came alive in great rolling waves, like waves on a great lake. The grass whipped and played a soft music with the wind.

Lewis patted my back, then helped me to my feet. "Listen; you can hear voices in the wind."

He was right. It was like murmurs and whispers.

"John's grandfather said they were the spirits of long ago hunters."

I found myself smiling.

"He said you never leave the land. The spirit remains."

"Do you believe that?" I said as I wiped my eyes.

Lewis looked at the swaying prairie, but I believed he was looking at something else that I could not see. A smile grew on his face. "We believed."

I looked across the prairie. I knew I didn't see what he saw.

"Some things you can't hold in your hands," Lewis said. "You can't see them with your eyes, but they are there all the same. You feel them and you know they are there. They make things happen out of your control."

"Like God," I said.

Lewis's smile grew.

We sat there for a long time not saying anything, just looking at the same prairie, but each seeing something different. Then I remembered the words John kept saying.

"Lewis, what does *Akki-Kni* mean?" Lewis picked up a big snail, inspected it, and flung it across the prairie. "It means 'to return home.'"

I smiled and nodded.

Lewis patted me on my shoulder. "Let us go back before Mr. Stilman worries over us."

The grass waved, and the prairie was alive as we headed back.

***

The next morning was very cool for late July. The weather would be our friend as we paddled upstream.

Mr. Stilman stood on the porch and held General Jackson with a rope as we said our goodbyes. "Come back down this way this fall, and we will hunt the big ole bucks that haunt these woods."

"Mr. Stilman, I want to thank you for your hospitality," Lewis said as we stepped off the porch.

"I've done nothing that amounted to anything for more years than I care to recall, just sat here and hid from the world. The little I did for y'all was more of a tonic for me."

Before we left the clearing that the little cabin sat in, I turned back to see Mr. Stilman rocking in his chair and scratching General Jackson behind the ear. I never saw either of them again.

***

I could smell the river long before we got to it, reminded me of home, and I was really starting to miss the farm and my family.

When we arrived at the river bank, the first thing I spotted was a very long canoe—Lewis's canoe. Lewis placed our bags into it.

"You gonna be able to paddle that thing against the current?" I said.

"Me and this old canoe have been up and down this river more times than you can count."

I grinned. "Well, we have to take the little pirogues back with us," I said. "They are tied behind those trees." When I went behind the trees, there was only one. John's was gone.

"I reckon John's been here," Lewis said.

John's bag was in that pirogue. "He left this," I said.

"If he left it, he wanted you to have it."

I opened it. There was the Red Eagle.

Lewis pulled the little pirogue to the water's edge and tied it behind his canoe. "Let's go."

"Why?"

Lewis shoved the boats into the water. "Why what?"

"He came all this way. He went through so much for it, and he just left it."

"I'm disappointed in you." Lewis got into the canoe, and I followed. We shoved off. The rope tightened and pulled the little pirogue behind the canoe. "John has a bow and full quiver of arrows now. He doesn't need the sinew to make string anymore."

I looked down at the bag. I understood and remembered what John had said, "You are me, John Gillette. You are me." The bag with the Red Eagle suddenly felt very heavy.

Chapter 11

"Pup, I never saw Lewis again after he delivered me to the farm," Mr. Gillette said, as he ran his wrinkled hand across the tablet An old truck rumbled down the street and smoke drifted across the park.

"What do you think happened to Lewis? What about Mr. Stilman?" I said.

The old man turned to me with a big grin spread across his lined face. His blue eyes twinkled with youth, but his body didn't cooperate. He squeezed my leg with a pretty good grip though.

"You like my story, Pup?"

"Yeah. Now tell me what happened to those old men."

He smiled. He knew he had me on a string. "Well, I tell you, I reckon that Mr. Stilman stayed right there on that porch until he died and turned to dust, never heard anymore about him."

"What about Lewis?"

The smile fell. He looked off across the park somewhere, but he wasn't looking at any one thing in particular. It was very strange. He said nothing.

I wanted to shake him. He was like an old clock that would just take a notion and stop ticking sometimes.

Still looking across the road, he started back. "Me and Pa went downstream to Maddox Bay about a month later. Pa had really acted queer when I told him my story about John and Lewis. He wanted to talk with Lewis, said he hadn't talked to him in many years. It was the first time I found out he even knew Lewis." Mr. Gillette stopped ticking again.

"Well?" I patted his leg. "Will you stop keeping me hanging!"

He turned and bore those blue eyes into mine. "When we went up into the bay, that old shanty was as abandoned as last year's bird nest."

"He had moved? What?" I said.

He shook his head slowly. "No, Pup; his stuff was still there, just like when I was last there."

I didn't understand. You don't move without taking your stuff. "Maybe you just missed him, and he was coming back."

"His fishing boat was there, but his canoe was gone. His spirit was gone—I could feel it. No, Pup; he was never coming back. It was strange. There were spiderwebs on everything, dust on everything."

I wanted to believe Mr. Gillette was pulling my leg, or he was just old; but I just didn't know. There was a strange chill running through me.

"Then an old colored man came a-paddling by as we were getting back into the boat. Pa asked him about Lewis."

"What did he say?"

Mr. Gillette rubbed his chin. "The man said he saw Lewis going down river in his long canoe about three or four weeks back. He said it was strange. Lewis looked different, had on buckskins."

I swallowed. Mr. Gillette had me hooked with the story now for sure.

"The colored man scratched his head and said, 'I could swear to Jesus he looked forty years younger.'" Mr. Gillette bent and tied his shoe. "That's what the man said."

"Did you believe the colored man?"

"Yeah, Pup, I believed him. I remembered the way he looked the night of the storm when he was standing outside the door."

Mr. Gillette's story was getting pretty strange. Now I was beginning to think he was pulling my leg.

"When me and Pa was in the cabin, we saw Lewis's musket laying across the table." He turned to me. "The old bow and arrows that hung above the fireplace were gone."

"That is strange," I said.

"We stopped on a sandbar before we made it back to the farm, the one with the kingfishers," Mr Gillette said. "Pa hadn't said two words to me since we left Maddox Bay. We sat on a drift log and talked man to man—something we had never done before then. He said he had known about John Gillette, said his father had told him all about him. He said his father had told him about the Red Eagle, but Pa hadn't believed it, hadn't believed any of it, so my grandfather stopped talking about it."

"Did your pa believe your story?" I said.

"Yeah. Yeah, he believed me. After my story he wiped his eyes and said he wished he had believed my grandfather. But he told me something that I still wrestle with to this day. He said a few weeks before I ran away, he had received a letter that John Gillette had died out west."

I felt the chill again. I said, "The letter must have been a mistake."

"Yeah, it must have been."

We sat there saying nothing for a long time. Then Mr. Gillette said, "It was all a sign from *Wah-Kon-Tah*."

"You've lost me, Mr. Gillette. What is *Wah-Kon-Tah*?"

"Damn, Pup. Didn't you listen to my story? It means 'the great spirit.'"

Sometimes the old man had little patience.

"Pa told me to never tell mother about any of it—I never did. Pa died a couple years later. Over the years I tried to tell a few friends, but no one believed me."

I was screwed up. I didn't know if the old man was pulling my leg or what.

Mr. Gillette placed a hand on my leg. "So you see, Pup, Lewis was right; the spirits roam the prairie. And no one believes my story, so the spirits are safe."

"What about the Red Eagle?"

Mr. Gillette got up from the bench. "What kinda eagle?" He looked across the street. "The movie's over, and the old folks are coming out. And look, they're like puppies looking for their momma." He smiled and pointed.

I got up from the bench, but I wanted more of the story. "Mr. Gillette, how did he—"

"Come on, Pup." Mr. Gillette started for the bus. "The old folks are waiting." He turned back and winked at me.

I watched the old man waddle toward the bus and mingle with the other old folks. I smiled, then laughed. I had been had by an old man. He snagged me, hook line and sinker. What a fool I was. I looked down at the tablet he had dropped to the ground. I picked it up and saw what he had been drawing. It was a red eagle. He really was an artist.

Chapter 12

October 1, 2015, Verizon Arena in North Little Rock Arkansas

I looked out across the arena—it was packed. It was not a rock concert, and it was no ballgame; yet, it was packed all the same. Big TV screens flickered everywhere for the poor souls too far away to see the stage. What a marvel of engineering the grand arena is.

There were people from all over the globe, all there for something good—something that actually made a difference on earth. It was great to know the world could be changed without a war—I've seen way too many wars. I had never seen anything like the event in my ninety-five years—and I've seen plenty.

The   chairman   of   the   society   stepped   up   to   the microphone. I forgot his name—I forget a lot now. But what I do know is he believes in what he is doing, to the core. They all believe or they would not have been there in that arena in North Little Rock.

"Ladies and Gentlemen, I want to sincerely, from the core of my heart, thank you for coming to our annual event," the chairman began his speech. "I want to start by simply saying at this very moment there are no two countries on this planet at war with each other."

Oh, how the crowd leaped to their feet and cheered. How they went on and on, made me so proud.

"The earth is now cleaner than it has been in a hundred years!"

The cheering hit a higher pitch.

As the crowd settled down, the chairman continued, "We have accomplished so much. We have changed the world for the good. We have made a difference!" He raised his arms. "You have made a difference! "

The cheering started up again and went on for ten minutes before the chairman could continue.

"We do not threaten for peace with war—it is not our way. We do not beg for peace like cowards." He paused and the crowd patiently waited. "We do not demand that anyone does anything." He put his hand over his heart. "We show our fellow man respect and understanding. We prove to our neighbor that we respect his opinion even if it is not our own. We appreciate his culture, which may be different from ours. We don't just look for it—we find common ground!"

The crowd was back on its feet for five minutes.

"We know we still have to police society. There are still going to be people who do evil. But we should not accept it as normal. We should not look the other way. We should never be deterred from our goal of respect, kindness, and understanding for our fellow man and the good for Mother

Earth!"

I thought the steel beams of the arena would buckle and fall from the roar of the crowd.

"Friends, we have accomplished so much with our simple ideas. We have made the earth a better place—not perfect, but better." He stopped and took a long pause before continuing. "Tonight I have a surprise for you. This movement had a beginning. One man had a vision."

The crowd cheered again. The chairman smiled and waited patiently for the roar to subside.

"It is my honor and privilege to welcome the founder of *The Society of the Red Eagle*—Glenn 'Pup' Goodwil."

As the crowd roared, my nephew helped me from my chair. I was proud and I felt so very alive. I walked to the microphone alone—I still had that much strength, but not much more.

The chairman shook my hand, careful not to squeeze too hard—he had been coached. He had heartfelt tears running down his cheeks, and I was moved.

The crowd roared louder than ever as I stepped up to the microphone. My nephew was afraid I could not stand there long enough to give my little speech, but I could have stood there until the end of days—which equaled only a few minutes.

"Friends." The crowd cheers faded as I began my little address. "Thank you for the welcome, but at my age I have to be brief."

The crowd laughed.

"I did not come before you to be honored, but to thank you. I came before you to honor you."

The crowed applauded.

"You all know me. You all know the story behind the organization. There are some that do not believe the story."

The crowd murmured and booed.

"Yeah, that's the way I feel, too."

The crowd laughed.

"Many have said the movement is what counts, not the story. I could not agree more. But I'm here to set the story straight."

There were halfhearted cheers from the crowd. They didn't know what to think. They had not expected it from me. I had been silent about the stories for so many years. Most didn't care about the story, only the deeds of the organization.

"Our society is based on belief: believe in each other, believe in the greater good, believe in your god or your spirit. You have to believe or nothing happens. We believe we can make a difference."

I reflected back to that day in Hot Springs on that park bench when John Gillette told me the story. Oh, how mixed up I was after that. I cursed the man and thanked the man. He had planned the whole thing. How many other times had he tried to plant that seed before me? How many people had brushed it off as a strange tale or him a nut?

He was so right about the war, and he was right about me going, too. Except I didn't fight Hitler's armies; the Pacific was my lot. And the seed he planted was nurtured on those hellish islands. War is hell—Sherman was right, the bastard. I never closed my eyes that I didn't dream of John's tale of the Red Eagle—the power of *Khi-Dha' Zhu'te*. I learned on those islands the power was not in that sculpture of red amber with the prehistoric creature trapped inside, for God only knows how long. The power was in believing. As long as you believe in something, there is a chance. As long as you try, it may happen. My whole company was wiped out, but I lived. I believed I would. I believed in God—my God. I lived. I believed—I believed...

My nephew took my arm. I turned and brushed him away.

I smiled so he would know I was fine. He went back to his seat.

I straightened my tired old frame as erect as I could. "Friends, I wanted you to believe. I want you to trust me. Do you trust me?"

The crowd assured me they did.

"Nothing will harm you here if you believe."

"We believe." The crowd chanted. "We believe."

"Always believe, friends—always believe," I said as I motioned to the man off stage.

A curtain was raised from a table to the right of me. All eyes were on the table. Slowly a dim spotlight lit the table, then another light, then another. The Red Eagle was revealed with all its splendor. Lights shown on it from every angle. Uplifting music blared from unseen speakers. The Red Eagle rotated like a diamond on a television commercial. It was flashed on every monitor in the area. The crowd was awed—they were shocked. There really was an actual Red Eagle!

"Do you believe?" I said.

They were not looking at me as an old man any longer. They saw me as a prophet—the Eagle an idol.

"Do you really believe?"

The arena shook with cheers. People cried and held their hands high in the air.

I motioned to the man off stage, and the lights went low.

"You must believe in yourself. You must believe you can make a difference. You must trust in what you believe."

Powerful strobe lights struck the Red Eagle—*Khi-Dha' Zhu'te*. The creature within came alive throughout the arena.

The crowd gasped as one.

The creature crawled across the arena as the strobe pulsed—a shadow, a ghost, a spirit. Each person later described it differently. Each person saw what they believed in. But this crowd was not afraid because they did believe. It was the power from their own god. It was from their own belief. They screamed. They prayed. They wept with a deep movement to the soul.

As suddenly as the strobe began; it stopped, and the lights came back on. A moan rolled throughout the arena.

It was the first time anyone had seen the creature since the night of the storm; the man operating the strobe didn't know what to expect. Even I had never seen it, but I had dreamed about it a million times, but too afraid to release it. I had faith that the strobe would reveal the creature for me and the world. I knew my time was growing near, and I had to finally do it. I had to finally be brave enough.

Slowly, one by one, each person held up a hand. They were in awe.

I stepped back to the microphone and took a deep breath. "This is not my god. This is not your god. Maybe it is a messenger; I don't know. I never understood. Maybe it's just science, but its powers meant something so many years ago, and promises were made that we can now keep." I raised my voice. "Promises to do good for all mankind and good for God's earth! Do you believe?"

A man way in the back shouted, "I believe." A few more joined in, then a few more, a few more still, until it was one voice: "I believe!" They did believe. The organization all believed as one. They all moved as one. They had found the sinew.

I turned to *Khi-Dha' Zhu'te*, thought of Mr. Gillette, not as an old man, but as a young man. He had done John's bidding, and now I had done his. What John, Paul, Charles, and Lewis could not do for the Quapaw, maybe we can do for the world. The prairies of Arkansas are no more, but I wager young John Gillette is in the beyond hunting in the tall grass with the other four believers, forever young. I squeezed the piece of shell in my pocket, whispered, "*Akki-Kni.*" My day is growing near, and I pray the spirits will let me join them on the Grand Prairie.

The End

Look for John Gschwend's first novel, *Chase The Wild Pigeons*, a Civil War novel like no other. See what others are saying about it:

"*...The triumph and terror these young boys faced during the civil war is unimaginable. I found myself cheering them on, almost crying for them. My heart broke, I laughed out loud and I was filled with anger and rage throughout the story. Not too many books can have people go through all those emotions and back again, but this one did...*" Courtney

"*...Two young adolescent boys, one white age 12, and one black age 16, become indelibly imprinted on your mind. Because this is a character-driven story, you laugh and you cry, you love and you hate, you react and you reflect. Gschwend's heart and soul resonate on every page. The story is action-packed. The description is superb...*" Edwynne.

"*Set in the deep south, Chase the Wild pigeons is a historically accurate novel that transports the reader back to the Civil War. The reader finds himself pulled into life on the Mississippi River, Southern culture and even Civil War era flora and fauna. Mr. Gschwend paints a vivid picture of the effects of war on a nation, especially from the stand point of a child. Chase the Wild Pigeons does a fine job of illustrating racial tensions across the south without being offensive, and tells a lovely story of two young men who have only each other to rely on. Entwined into this entertaining story is adventure, one that makes it difficult to put down. I read this book into the wee hours of the night! I highly recommend this book!*" Jenn Bryant

http://civilwarnovel.com

21121746R00099

Made in the USA
Charleston, SC
08 August 2013